ROSES *in*
the MINES

Other books by the author

Fear Not, Child (2014)

ROSES *in the* MINES

GABRIEL S. MAKERI

WORDS
RHYMES &
RHYTHM

Printed and Published in Nigeria by:
Words Rhymes & Rhythm Limited
Suite C309, Global Plaza Plot 366, Obafemi Awolowo
Way, Jabi District, Abuja, Nigeria.
08169027757, 08060109295
www.wrr.ng

for

Late J. B. D. Pam,

Mr. D. A. Iliya

and

Late Michael Auta

Through them, I was employed into the Ministry by the grace of God.

ACKNOWLEDGEMENTS

Gladys Asabe Goje (Mrs.)and Mr. Charles Osakwe for editing the work;Engr. M. K. Amate, Engr. Dauda A. Awojobi, K. F. Wuyep, Acting Director, Mines, Alhaji Sani Shehu, President, Miners' Association of Nigeria, all my principals in Mines Inspectorate Department, (bear with me for not listing your names here), all those who commented on this work as appeared in this book, Bature Mohammmed Gwani, Abunumah S. U and Eguro G. Makeri for your support.

I am also grateful to Mr. Emmanuel Edwin and Mr. Itopa Ibrahim for being patient in typing the manuscript and its corrections severally.

The names of persons, apart from those of past Mines Officers of old mentioned in remembrance of their exploits and those used by Engr. Sluice in testing his staff in the last chapter (including Alhaji Hassan Abduulmumin), and places used in the book are fictitious. Names of organizations, (excluding Iss-Hass Nig. Ltd and Tongyi Allied Mining Company) departments, and designations are fictitiously used in this novel. Any coincidence is not intentional whatsoever.

COMMENTS

"This book is a testimony to a well-spent 35 years in public service that has touched the well-being of the less privileged citizens who struggle for survival through hard labour of subsistence mining practice. I also found it to be a "function of reality," probably the best and only way of communicating the extant laws that regulate their unstoppable activities."

— **Professor Ibrahim Garba**, *Vice Chancellor, Ahmadu Bello University (ABU), Zaria, and former Director-General, Mining Cadastre Office (MCO)*

ಚಿ‍ೞ

"The book is very interesting. It provides a wealth of hard-to-find information on the activities of illegal miners in Nigeria as well as how they can form a mining co-operative and operate within the ambit of the law, and to benefit from various government programmes aimed at assisting artisanal and small scale mining operations."

— **Engr. B. O. Nwude**, *FNSME, FNSE, FNMGS, FAutoEI, Former President, Nigeria Society of Mining Engineers (NSME)*

ಚಿ‍ೞ

"The rose is a beautiful flower...yet surrounded by thorns...this is akin to the rich minesfield of Nigeria, full of riches in its deep belly yet shrouded with thorny issues that are tricky to navigate to the uninitiated....with this masterpiece, Makeri has outdone himself in depicting what is sometimes the tedious task of understanding the Mining Laws of Nigeria to a simple and flowery expose so enjoyable and frankly so 'unputdownable.' It is highly recommended for all,whether in the Mining industry or not."

— **Mr. Charles Osakwe**, *Executive Director, Logistics & Infrastructure,Owukpa Consolidated Mines Limited*

ಚಿ‍ೞ

"*Roses in the Mines* by Makeri, one of the front liners among the students I taught in Nigeria premier mining institution, the then Federal School of Mines,... reminds me of the topic I gave their class to discuss: *'The most important thing that comes out of the mine is the miner.'* Makeri is awfully painstakingly like the typical Japanese who gives attention to details. The book is worth reading. I must congratulate my mentee, Makeri, for this book."

— **Professor John Ade Ajayi**, *Federal University of Technology, Akure (FUTA)*

ഈറദ

"The novel encapsulates real time experience as a staff of Mines Inspectorate Department of the Ministry of Mines and Steel Development in relation to the Nigerian Minerals and Mining Act, 2007 and its Regulations of 2011. It is highly refreshing and educative."

— **Engr. Dauda Aremu Awojobi**, *FNSME, FNMGS, MNSE, COREN, COMEG, former Director, Mines Inspectorate Department*

"...an excellent piece, first of its kind. It can be comfortably and conveniently be converted and developed into a mining code for the mining sector."

— **Karnap Fenan Wuyep** *-Ag. Director, Mines Inspectorate*

ഈറദ

"*Roses in the Mines* is very captivating and educative. Makeri has explained the laws in a way that the layman can easily understand them. The use of the first language (L1), in this case, *Hausa* and *Pidgin English*, makes it easy for the reader to identify with the characters. There is a need for the average Nigerian to understand the laws and his rights to be protected against the side effects of all forms of mining activities. I, therefore, recommend this text to all Nigerians."

— **Gladys Asabe Goje (Mrs)**, *Language Department, Kaduna Polytechnic*

ഈറദ

"Honestly, the book is a well packaged piece that should be a companion to current Mines Officers and future ones. It will help them in the performance of their duties, as usual encounters in the mines fields and how they can be dealt with in accordance with the law are almost all captured. It is first of its kind in the Mines Inspectorate. Congrats."

— **Engr. Donatus Uba Umaru**, *Zonal Mines Officer, South West Zone*

"This book is a barrel of wisdom and knowledge packaged and presented in an atmosphere for an understanding and application of laymen and every other individual. It can also be used as a referral material by academicians, students, industry players, regulators, practitioners, and other stakeholders. It is therefore highly recommended."

— **Engr. Omoijuanfo Ihase S.O**, *Zonal Mines Officer, South-South Zone*

೮ಿ೮ಿ

"...easy to read and comprehend; an enlightening instrument to those who are ignorant of the architectures of the mining industry."

— **Engr. Habila Dauda**, *former Federal Mines Officer, Bauchi State*

೮ಿ೮ಿ

"The literature is well researched and informative. In fact, it will go a long way to clear some of the ambiguities in the mines fields."

— **Engr. Ayuba Ishaya** *(COREN), former Federal Mines Officer, Nasarawa State*

೮ಿ೮ಿ

"The Author, who is a Veteran of the mines fields, has shown us the resilience and the instinct for survival of both the miners and the Mines Officers in their daily activities. He has comically presented very serious issues that sometimes border on life and death. The book should be translated and dramatized for Extension Services outreach and be given the widest coverage to other ASM countries.This is our own *Mine Boy* and should be adopted by WAEC, NECO etc."

— **Rufus Gbenosa, MTech.**, *PGDE, Extension Services Officer, ASM Dept. Headquarters, MMSD, Abuja*

"This is a bold attempt to package the mining industry in a manner that will definitely appeal to all shades of the reading public. The author congregated his experiences in the mines fields into this masterpiece that will sustain the awareness drive in the mining sector for a long time to come."
— **Engr. Korie I. Ebere**, *former Federal Mines Officer, Imo State*

∞⌘

"The book is enlightening and timely because it sheds light on how to tackle the challenges encountered in the mines fields as a result of ignorance."
— **Engr. Isaac Gimba**, *former Federal Mines Officer, Sokoto State*

∞⌘

"This book epitomizes real experiences in the minesfields. I recommend it to every Mining Engineer."
— **Abunumah S.U**, *Federal Mines Officer, Zamfara State*

∞⌘

"*Roses in the Mines* is an appetizer to individuals, researchers, and potential investors in the Solid Minerals Sector. It is an eye-opener to the novice."
— **Engr. Jonathan Nwankwo**, *Mines Inspectorate Dept., Headquarters, Abuja*

"Our ambition goes beyond just extraction and exportation. We aim to create a globally competitive sector capable of contributing to wealth creation, jobs creation and the advancement of our social and human security. It is also to create a new culture of sustainable natural resource management that results in a win-win situation for all of us – communities, partners, and investors at home and abroad"

— **Minister of Mines and Steel Development, Dr. Kayode Fayemi**

(from an article titled **Nigeria Open for investment,** *published on the Ministry of Mines & Steel Dev website www.minesandsteel.gov.ng/ on May 23 2016)*

ONE

It was in an illegal gold mining camp, Zumunci Mining Camp, somewhere in Kebbi State, North West Zone of Nigeria, one cloudy Friday afternoon in the month of April that a man in his early seventies came out of a loto hole with reddish mud all over his body and drops of sweat streaming down his forehead. It seemed as if a bucket of water had been poured over him. But it was, indeed, sweat, salty sweat, as a result of hard work under high humidity and limited ventilation in the loto hole.

The man sat under the shade of a fruitless tree. Many birds were on it at the time, merrily jumping from branch to branch and chirping. He recalled an encounter he and other illegal miners had had with Mines Officers two years ago in an illegal mining camp in the South West Zone of Nigeria. The Mines Officers had advised them – the illegal miners, on the need to formalise their operations so that they could enjoy extension services from the Government as provided in Section 91 of the Nigerian Minerals and Mining Act of 2007 (to be hereafter simply referred to as the "Act" unless otherwise stated). He remembered they told them about a Small Scale Mining Lease (SSML) but he had forgotten its maximum area which is 15 Cadastral Units (CUs), the equivalent of 3.0375 Square Kilometers. However, he remembered he was told that an applicant for a mineral title of that category could take even less than that, even one Cadastral Unit (0.2025 Square Kilometer). He recalled having been told before that there is an agency of the Ministry of Mines and Steel Development (MMSD), Mining Cadastre Office (MCO), that is responsible for

1

the administration of mining land titles or mineral titles as some would call. He wished he could convince his colleagues, the informal miners, to come together and form a mining co-operative. This would make them free from the periodic harassment from the Mines Officers of the Mines Inspectorate Department (MID) of the MMSD who supervise mining operations and enforce compliance with the provisions of the Act and the Nigerian Minerals and Mining Regulations, 2011 (to be hereafter simply referred to as the 'Regulations' unless otherwise stated). It was while he was deeply thinking on this that his mobile phone, a rugged Nokia brand of low quality, rang. As if he was expecting the call, he immediately removed it from the pocket of the trousers he wore and listened to the caller and then exclaimed:

"Find of Gold! Gold! Gold in Zamfara State! Let us go now!" He said to other illegal miners and began to pick his work tools – a hammer, a digger, a head-pan and a guard of *kunu*, getting ready to go. Other illegal miners were also excited and ready to go with him. They respected him so much because his demeanor was that of innocence and he had the aura of royalty around him. He cared for them all without discrimination. A story has it that he had been an old miner since the time the Germans mined gold in Tsohon Birnin Gwari in Kaduna State until they unwillingly and hurriedly left at the advent of the Second World War. He had related how the Germans hurriedly dug a big hole, put many things in it, covered it, cemented all its top, deposited top soil on it and planted trees on the spot, hoping to return after the war to retrieve those buried items which no doubt could be gold dust or nuggets. Surely, this worldwide cherished precious metal, one of the treasures of the

Universe, could be the primary reason for which the hole was dug in the first instance. It is hoped one day this great treasure would be found by the government to boost the Nigerian economy.

It was in this excited and maddening rush to leave the Zumunci Mining Camp - and that is the way of their life; they are always moving, always moving from one illegal mining camp to another in search of gold and the gems, as news of new and rich discoveries spread - that one Kehinde Adesina and some people arrived. A Mining Engineer, Adesina was the Technical Competent Person, as stipulated in Section 73(1) of the Act and Section 26 of the Regulations, for the mining company which had a mineral title over the Zumunci Mining Camp. He came with a man wearing mining kits, his supporting staff and six policemen. A heavily built Sergeant Donald who walked like the solders of old fighting in the jungles of Congo was the leader of the policemen and the rest were all Corporals. All were dressed in combat wears. They came on a surveillance mission.

The illegal miners started to run away out of fear in different directions, throwing away their work implements and some items among which were sticks of gelatin, lengths of dynacords, safety fuses and pieces of plain detonators they had illegally acquired against the provisions of Section 2(c) of the Explosives Act, 1964 and Section 3 of the Explosives Regulations, 1967. These contain the laws that guide the manufacturing, possession, use, buying, sales and conveying of commercial explosives.

It was not only the illegal miners that started running; traders of different goods, women of easy virtue and a couple of illegal marital unions also did. However, they were not many as the mining site was not promising for the traces of gold already found did not point to the occurrence of a rich deposit in the area. The rush of the illegal miners to the area was minimal unlike the rush sometime in 2006 to the site of Alhaji Hassan Abdulmumin, the Chairman of Iss-Hass Nigeria Limited, at Garin Auwal which is a remote but attractive and dignified local settlement in Kebbi State.

"Jemi!Jemi! My money! Give me my money," a woman called out to an illegal miner called James who owed her money. James had been eating on credit from her for the past two weeks with the hope of paying her when he succeeded in getting and selling some gold dust. If James ran away to another mining camp, possibly not to Zamfara State, it would be difficult for the woman to get her money. It was possible they would not meet again. Some other traders were also heard calling at their debtors as they, too, were trying to run away. But who would listen to them in such a moment of anxiety and confusion?

"*Aaaaa; yaya ta na tunanin ina da kudi in ba ta yanzun* (Goodness; how does she think I have the money to give her now)?" James was heard saying, hanging his bag on his shoulder, getting ready to run.

Some of the illegal miners were seen coming out of loto holes, almost masked by reddish mud to run for safety but they would not go far.

"Nobody should run away! If you do, we will open fire on you! Come back or...," Sergeant Donald ordered, cocking his gun, ready to shoot. They obeyed and stopped running, fearful of what might happen to them. Some were seen with some powdery substance. It was gold dust; the substance of their sweat and happiness.

"Everybody should bring any weapon in his possession whether it is an ordinary stick or stone and lay it down here. Don't let me say this for the second time," Sergeant Donald said, pointing at the spot where the weapons were to be laid. His face was rigid, showing no sign of joke but ridges of frowns all over. He moved without looking down at lumps of soil under his feet that could make him lose his balance.

"Even a gun? Where did you get it, dangerous old man?" Sergeant Donald asked. It was the old man who had just announced the discovery of gold at a location in Zamfara State.

On preliminary interrogation, the old man revealed that he had picked the gun some months ago in the bush of Zamfara State in the vicinity of Dansadau in the course of illegal mining. Sergeant Donald remembered having been told of police encounters with cattle rustlers and armed bandits in that area and believed it could have been thrown away by one of them when they were pursued.

"But why didn't you report to the Police Station with the gun since then? Anyway, you will explain this in the Station when we get there," Sergeant Donald said and directed the Corporals to handcuff him. He resisted like a stubborn cow about to be killed in an abattoir but he was overpowered. "Stupid old man; loosen yourself if you think you can," one of the Police Corporals said.

"I am surprised, Sergeant," Kehinde Adesina said, looking fearful. He had been going there without suspecting there could be somebody with a gun.

"Since you obeyed, instead of justice in accordance with the mining laws it will be mercy but you should not come here again. I hope *Oga* will accept this," Sergeant Donald said, feeling sorry for them as he saw poverty written all over their faces. The *Oga* he was referring to was the man in the mining kits who was still looking at the scattered loto holes that had been dug, wondering how a mine design for such a devastated area would come up.

"Sergeant, *babamu, kai muke so* (Sergeant, our father, it is you we like)!" Uban Daba, the leader of the illegal mining camp, said, laughing.

"Shut up and listen," one of the Corporals shouted at Uban Daba, surging towards him with a raised hand, ready to slap him. He did not hear Hausa and therefore could not understand him. He thought it was nasty words he said to Sergeant Donald. Sergeant Donald stopped the zealous Corporal and laughed at his ignorance.

"Sergeant, za *ka sha taba* (Sergeant, will you smoke)?" Uban Daba asked, stretching a stick of cigarette and a lighter to him and sending into the air a column of smoke from his nostrils while at the same time, throwing a stick of cigarette he had not finished smoking to the ground. He matched on it with his leg to quench the fire, exhibiting one of the habits of smokers.

"Do you see me as a smoker? Don't talk again until you are permitted. Do you hear me?" he said and warned him not to smoke again until the meeting was over as he knew that passive smoking also kills.

"*Chan*, sir; Okay, sir, *Oga kenan*," Uban Daba said, laughing and said to the rest, "*kowa ya yi shiru; ku sani muna da dokoki anan* (everybody should be quiet, you know we have rules here)."

"All of you sit down," Sergeant Donald instructed so as to feel more secured. All this while, the man in the mining kits who had a commanding presence had been quiet. "This man," Sergeant Donald continued and pointed at the man in the mining kits, "is the Inspector of Mines in-charge of the North-West zone. He is going round the zone to see what is happening in the mines fields. He will address you now; listen to him quietly; no noise. Corporals ensure this, please," he concluded, giving the chance to the Inspector of Mines and beckoned Uban Daba to come to him. He whispered some words into his ears.

"I greet all of you," the Inspector of Mines began, waving his hands as if he was practicing the art of speech delivery he had read somewhere.

"*Sonu da zuwa, Oga* (you are welcome, Boss)", some of the illegal miners responded, fixing their eyes probingly on him, hoping they would not be rounded up and taken to the Police Station and wraps of their gold dust seized.

"Once again," the Inspector of Mines continued, "I greet all of you. I am Engineer Russo Sluice. I am here with my team to educate you on the Nigerian mining laws," he continued and turned to Sergeant Donald and asked whether all of them could understand him in English. About seventy percent of them could neither hear nor speak English very well.

"Continue, sir," Sergeant Donald said and assigned one man whom he knew to interpret the highlights in Hausa language. The man had dropped out of school when he was in his first year in the university due to circumstances beyond his control.

"Uban Daba, *akwai Manir da Dankano a rami fa. Kuna ji kara hamarsu? Ba su san abinda ke faruwa ba* (Uban Daba, Manir and Dankano are in the hole. Do you hear the sound of their hammer? They don't know what is happening)," one of the illegal miners interrupted by drawing their attention.

"Keep quiet," Sergeant Donald ordered.

7

"*Some persons still dey inside one hole digging the stone for the gold. They no know say una come*," Uban Daba tried to explain in English.

"What is he saying?" Engr. Sluice asked Sergeant Donald. He was from the South West and was just trying to learn how to speak the Hausa language.

"Sir, he said there are some people who are still in one of the holes, working."

"Where?" Engr. Sluice asked, with his mouth ajar.

"Can you hear the sound of a hammer *for* that place?" Uban Daba asked Engr. Sluice, pointing at the direction from which the sound was coming, his hand shaking as a result of intensive smoking and drinking of alcohol over the years.

"Sergeant, let us go there with Baba Dabam (he meant Uban Daba). Corporals, stay here. Make sure nobody misbehaves; okay?" Engr. Sluice said, leaving for the hole with fury as if he would go and swallow them; but he was not a python.

ℰ☭

"Who are you? Come out or I shoot!" Sergeant Donald threatened, pointing the gun beyond the collar of the hole.

"Manir, Dankano, *duk guje-guje da surutu da mu yi ba ku ji ba* (Manir, Dankano, did you not hear all the running and the noise we made)? *Ku yi lura* (be careful)," Uban Daba called and spoke to them, bending and looking into the hole and gradually slipping towards the hole as the excavated heap of soil upon which he stood was not stable.

"*Me ke faruwa ne* (what is it that is happening)?" Dankano asked and told Manir to keep on working.

"*Don Allah da Anebi, ku fito da sauri* (because of God and the Prophet, come out quickly)," Uban Daba pleaded and asked Sergeant Donald to lend him a helping hand to avoid slipping further and finally into the hole.

"Come out quickly or I shoot you! Don't be foolish!" Sergeant Donald continued to threaten and dropped small quantity of soil into the hole to show his seriousness.

"*Uban Daba, ka fara ko? Don me ka sauko mana kasa?* (Uban Daba, have you started again? Why did you drop soil on us?)," Manir spoke.

"*Ba ni ba ne!* Police *ne! Fito!* (It is not I! It is police! Come out!)," Uban Daba Spoke.

"*Polisawa suna damu mu* (Police are disturbing us)," Dankano was heard complaining.

"What is Polisawa?" Sergeant Donald asked.

"*Na so* we *dey* call *una for* North. Polisawa na plenty police, pass one," Uban Daba answered and asked him, "*sebi* you say you stay for North before-before?"

"Bush man, if I had stayed in the North before, must I know everything? Tell your brothers to come out or I will waste them inside the hole."

"Manir, *ku fito. Me ya sa kuna taurarawa haka?* (Manir, you should come out. What makes you to so stubborn?)," Uban Daba spoke to them, fearing that the worst might happen if the Sergeant's patience reached its limit.

"*Za mu fito* (we will come out)," they said. As they threatened Manir and Dankano, they overheard a Corporal shouting.

※

"Where are you going? Sit down or I shoot you!" one of the Corporals shouted at three illegal miners who stood up. From all indications, they wanted to run away. There was an upheaval as many of them stood up, ready to fight the Policemen and the supporting Mines Officers. Some of them started heading towards the laid down weapons for a pick.

"If you pick any weapon, we will shoot you!" one of the Corporals said, cocking his gun. They could not listen and the police sporadically shot into the air to scare them. They had not been given order to shoot at sight.

※

"*Me ke faruwa ne*? (What is it that is happening?)" Uban Daba asked from the top of his voice, telling Sergeant Donald and Engr. Sluice that they should go back and see what was happening before they come back for Manir and Dankano. Before they arrived, the Corporals had quieted the rebellion. However, from the sporadic shooting, a bullet landed on the foot of a young boy, little Joe, 15 years old. The bullet pierced through the foot into the soil.

※

"*Wetin* happen, Femi?" Uban Daba asked. Femi was his assistant in running the camp.

"*Na* this kunama that said people should run away. I warned him but... but he refused to listen to me. Many decided to follow his stupid advice and began to quarrel with the Policemen and they shoot randomly into the air. Look at what has happened now; little Joe's foot is now bad," Femi explained, pointing at little Joe. Little Joe was an orphan who had dropped out of school because he could not pay the school fees. He decided to join the illegal miners so as to raise money to go back to school. His late father had mined gold in Laka in the vicinity of Birnin Yauri in Kebbi State. Unfortunately, the gods of the minerals did not smile favourably on him and he died poor, leaving the family in shear lack that was yet to be broken.

"You, kunama, you *no dey* hear word," Femi continued and surged towards him and beat him, exhibiting how embittered he was.

"So, you are the kunama? *Banja mutane* (stupid people), come here!" Sergeant Donald ordered. It was *banza mutum* (stupid person) he wrongly said *banja mutane* as he was greatly handicapped in the Hausa language.

"*Wannan soko ya na lalatar mana yare* (this foolish person is spoiling our language)," one of the illegal miners said. The people laughed.

"Why are they laughing?" Engr. Sluice asked.

"No *froblem*, sir," Uban Daba said.

"Keep quiet," Sergeant Donald ordered. "Kunama, you wanted to fight my people? Who gave you the audacity to do that?"

Kunama tried to speak.

"Shut up! You *akuya* (goat)," Sergeant Donald ordered and told the Corporals to handcuff him. He too would be taken to the police station. "All of you should lie flat on your bellies; Corporals!"

"Yes, sir."

"You know what to do. Anybody who tries to be funny, wound him," he ordered but he silently reminded them that they had not been ordered to kill.

11

They were there to educate illegal miners to formalize their mining activities.

The government is aware that these informal miners are also informal geologists that help in some new discoveries of mineral deposits although they are not professionals and, therefore, are technically handicapped.

"Engr. Sluice," Sergeant Donald called, "let us go back to those stupid boys in the hole," he said and beckoned Uban Daba to follow them. They got to the place.

ഏരു

"Manir! Dankano! *Fito!* (Come out)!" Uban Daba said, bending over the loto hole. He could not hear any sign of human presence. He dropped some coarse grains of soil into the hole. There was no complaint from Manir and Dankano as before. A lump of loose soil was dropped into the hole but still there was no complaint or groaning heard.

"You guys, what do you suppose might have happened?" Engr. Sluice, the Inspector of Mines, asked. He removed a Global Positioning System (GPS) from his pocket and took the co-ordinates of the hole.

"*Wadanan mutane ba su sani ba.* Manir *da* Dankano *sun riga sun fito sun gudu sa'anda sun taho nan* (these people do not know, Manir and Dankano have come out and run away when they were coming here)," one of the illegal miners, a seemingly composed man, whose constitution seemed to contain sharp intellect, said and laughed lightly. He saw the time they came out from another hole, some distance away from where Engr. Sluice, Sergeant Donald and Uban Daba were standing. It was later discovered that the two holes had been interconnected through a lateral tunnel created by stopping a poor vein of the gold deposit.

"Uban Daba! Uban Daba! Manir *da* (and) Dankano *sun riga sun fito sun gudu tuntuni*! (have come out and ran away for long)," the man who had seen them spoke in a loud voice.

"What is he saying?" Engr. Sluice asked Uban Daba, looking frustrated.

"He *be infom* me say *dem* already *comot* and run away when we go to find the matter for the people quarrelling with the Corporals," Uban Daba explained with his raw English. That did not concern him; at least he could be understood. That was the joy of Engr. Sluice and Sergeant Donald.

"The day I get them they will smell pepper. They don't know me," Sergeant Donald said in anger and asked them to go back where the Corporals were with the people. But even if he would come across them one day, how would he know they were the persons that ran away since he had not seen them?

As they were going, Engr. Sluice slipped into one of the scattered loto holes that had been dug all over a reasonably large area. If not for his safety kits, the boots and the helmet, it would have been very bad for him. Another thing that helped him was that the hole was not yet deep. It was just above his height and with a single bench. He came out of it unharmed.

"*Sori* (Sorry), Engineer. *Allah*, you are very *loki* (lucky) the hole no deep well-well. *Wallahi* (Honestly), you for break your neck. *Mun gode Allah* (we thank God)," Uban Daba said while dusting up Engr. Sluice.

"Sorry, Engr. Sluice. No wound?" Sergeant Donald sympathized and asked while trying to conceal laughter.

"No, Sergeant. Thank you, Baba Dabam," Engr. Sluice responded and they continued to move to meet the Corporals and the people.

TWO

"Tell all of them to quickly be on their feet. The Inspector of Mines will address them now," Sergeant Donald ordered the Corporals. He then turned to Uban Daba and said, "Tell your men to keep quiet and listen very well." Uban Daba complied.

"Sir, you can now address them," Sergeant Donald told the Inspector of Mines.

"Once again, I greet all of you; it is regrettable that we were interrupted by the unfortunate behavior of Manir and Dankano. I sincerely regret that we could not get them because of your bad behavior that made us to leave their hole to come and find out what was happening. Let me be very clear to all of you, nobody should ever attempt to misbehave again. If you do, it will not be good for all of you," Engr. Sluice said and turned to look at a Corporal who was telling one of the illegal miners to keep quiet. The illegal miner was quarrelling with his colleague and attempted to wrestle him down. His colleague had lied to him that while they were trying to run away when the Inspector of Mines with his team arrived, he lost some gold dust they both owned. The illegal miner did not believe him and the quarrelling ensued. That is how they are sometimes very mischievous. The group does usually comprise not of sluggish, but smart and scheming people.

"What is it Corporal?" Engr. Sluice asked. The Corporal turned to answer him and suddenly, the illegal miner, like a lion ambushing a prey, pounced on his colleague in judo style, pushing him down.

"Stop that nonsense!" Sergeant Donald ordered, rushing to separate them. Unfortunately, one of his legs got hooked by the loose root of a shrub that had not been completely detached from its mother source. He fell down and his already cocked gun fired. But nobody was wounded. This surprised everybody; divinity had intervened.

When he discovered nobody was wounded, he stood up and shouted again, "Will you not stop that nonsense!" By this time, the illegal miner was already on top of his colleague, beating and searching his pocket.

"What is this? Is it not the gold dust? Liar! Cheat! You can't do that to me," the illegal miner said, panting heavily and unloosening the wrap of the gold dust, telling everybody that his colleague had lied to him that it had been lost.

"Sergeant, collect that gold dust. Anybody that has gold dust with him should bring it out. Don't allow me to ask the police to search your pockets," Engr. Sluice spoke. Many complied but some had to be forced through the checking of their pockets. All wraps of gold dust were collected and Engr. Sluice referred them to Section 146 of the Act that sanctions the seizure of work tools, implements, vehicles and illegally won minerals. He told them Section 20 of the Regulations gives effect to this.

"*Aikin mu ya zama banza* (Our effort has becomes useless)," a friend to Kunama remarked.

"*Dogo, ka fara kuma ko? Kana so a yi maka kamar aka yi abokinka, kunama ko* (Dogo, you have started again? Do you want them to deal with you like they dealt with your friend, Kunama)?" Uban Daba spoke, trying to maintain silence and peace.

"Uban Daba, *zan bata maka rai yanzun in ba ka kiyaye kan ka ba* (if you are not careful I will make

16

you unhappy)," Dogo warned, ready to rebelliously move away from the gathering.

"Where are you going?" Sergeant Donald asked Dogo and told him to stay or he would face the consequences. He obeyed and looked at Uban Daba in bitterness. He was one of the people that made the camp difficult for Uban Daba to manage. Sometimes, Uban Daba had to plead with them. They were powerful determinants of events in the camp and no successful leader ignored them.

"I am not happy with all of you. Can you not just be courteous in my presence? What manner of people are you? Nonsense; we are trying to be merciful to you and yet you are being stupid. That must not be repeated," Engr. Sluice, the Inspector of Mines, spoke and continued to address them, "We are here to enlighten you on the laws that govern the mining of minerals in this great country, Nigeria. They are embodied in the Act and the Regulations. The Government of the Federation takes care of all minerals and controls their mining for the benefit of all Nigerians as provided for in Section 1(1) of the Act. You get me?"

"Yes, sir!" those that heard English responded.

"*Menene ya fada* (what did he say)?" One of the men who had never gone to school asked. During the time of intensive mining of casiterite and columbite in the Plateaus, he was employed by one European conglomerate and now he could say much on casiterite and columbite as if he had been schooled in them.

"*Ya nuna damursa akan abinda ya faru yanzun da cewa kada wannan ya sake faruwa kuma. Ya kuma ce sun zo ne don fahimta da mu cewa ma'adanai wannan kasar Nijeriya na karkashin*

17

gwananti taraya ne a madadin dukan yan Nijeriya bias ga dokokin na ma'adanai." The interpreter explained to him what Engr. Sluice had said.

"*Ayohhhhh, na gani* (Ohhhhh, I understand)," the man said and whispered into the ear of the interpreter.

"What did he whisper to you?" Engr. Sluice asked.

"Sir, he said you are a good man and that he wants to hear English Language but it is too late for him," he lied because the man told him that Engr. Sluice had a big stomach.

"Forget about him, who asked him not to go to school?" he said on a lighter mood, silently and ignorantly appreciating the man for labeling him a good man and advised that a summary of his address be given after he was done. He continued with the address.

"Nobody is allowed to give anybody permission to mine the minerals apart from the Federal Government through the Mining Cadastre Office which is administered by a Director-General who is under the Minister. Even a State Government or a Local Government cannot give you licence to mine minerals anywhere. Section 1(3) says minerals should be lawfully won in accordance with the provisions of the Act.

"You people may say only big companies can get a licence to mine minerals. No! The government knows your importance to the economy and the social security of this country and has allowed the formation of mining co-operatives to capture your category, the artisanal miners, fully into the design of the mining laws. This is provided in Section 91 of the Act.

"The Artisanal and Small Scale Mining (ASM) Department as provided for in Section 91 of the Act, was created to help you people in your mining activities by providing extension services to you. Your type of mining is limited to mineralized zones according to Section 90(3) of the Act.

"This place has been Licenced to Messers Mining for Nigeria Progress Plc, an indigenous company," Engr. Sluice continued and turned, asking for Kehinde Adesina, "Where is Engr. Adesina?" Engr. Adesina moved forward. "This young man is the Mining Engineer for the company," he introduced him to them. "Adesina, where is that copy of your Exploration Licence?"

"Here is it, sir," he brought it out of a folder.

"Give it to me," he collected it and raised it up for all to see.

"Can all of you see it?"

"Yes, *Oga*."

"This is the Licence over this area. You are therefore advised to form your own mining co-operative and apply for your area of interest to formalize your mining activities as provided for in Section 222 of the Regulations."

"Everywhere we go they say somebody or one company has a Licence over it. What do they want us to do? To go and steal? *Haba*," one of the illegal miners complained and turned his back in anger, walking away from the meeting. He had just come to the site two days ago from an illegal mining camp in Bauchi where illegal miners were recently raided. He was lucky to have run away. Many that were caught were undergoing prosecution.

19

"Who is talking over there? Keep quiet! Don't be stubborn. How many times shall we warn all of you?" Sergeant Donald spoke.

"Bulldozer," Uban Daba called, "keep quiet. Why you *no dey* hear word? *Haba, menene ku ke?Anan ce ku yi shuru,ba ku yi ba* (Oh, no, what are you? You are asked to keep quiet and you don't). I *no* like this." He is called Bulldozer because he could sink a loto hole even in hard ground to a great depth in a short time. "*Cigaba, Oga* (Continue, Boss)," he said, looking embarrassed.

"If you get your site, you can formalize your mining activities in compliance with Section 222 of the Regulations and begin to enjoy extension services. But for now, you will have to vacate this place because when next we come here, we shall not be lenient. Is that clear?"

"Yes, sir," some of them said while some murmured. The interpreter summarized the Inspector of Mines' address quickly.

"Tell them if they have questions, I am ready to answer them," Engr. Sluice told Sergeant Donald.

"We have many questions, so many of them," Bulldozer said and raised his hand up.

"Yes, ask your question," but he vacillated.

"Bulldozer, ask your question. We, too, have questions to ask," one illegal miner, Kunle, spoke.

"Kunle, if you talk again, I will bulldoze you, you know me," Bulldozer said, pointing his hand at him.

"Ask the question and stop that nonsense," Sergeant Donald said.

"*Oga*, Inspector for mineral, my boss, no, our boss; I am happy to meet you today," Bulldozer began.

"Go straight to your question, many people have questions to ask," Dogo joined.

"*Oga*, tell us small about this *una* (your) mining co-operative; how *e bi* (is it)?" Bulldozer finally asked.

"This is an appropriate question; you seem to be very intelligent," Engr. Sluice said. "You know *say* you people be what we *dey* call informal miners who *dey* mine minerals illegally and anyhow without machines like bulldozer, excavator, air compressor, drilling machine and others like that because you *no* get power in term of money to buy them and because your operation *dey* small, we call it small scale mining. As you *no* fit get big money to buy the machines and to get Licence for the mining like the millionaires or the billionaires, *na im* (that is why) government have pity on *una* and think say it should allow *una* to come together and form groups and register yourselves as co-operative societies. Section 222 of the Regulations is about this. After you register your co-operative with the State Government, you *go* now come to our Ministry where there is one big department for *una* category. *Den dey* call *am* Artisanal and Small Scale Mining (ASM) Department. It was established in accordance with the provisions of Section 16(1)(c) of the Act. *Una go* register the co-operative society with this Department *say* you be want do mining. This makes you all round Mining Co-operative. When you get your Small Scale Mining Lease (SSML) to work according to the Mining Act and the Regulations, *una don* become formalized and no more harassment for una. *Ehen*, keep quiet; one thing *e be* say your trustees or leaders for the mining co-operative should not be less than ten persons *wey be say dem no go* cheat *una*. Another thing also *e be say* government wants you people to gain well-well for this small scale mining and so *dey don* provide for *una* what we called extension services. The whole story on this good thing for *una* from the government is found in Section 223 of the Regulations. *Ego* better for my staff to read *am* so that *una* hear *am*," he said and turned to one of his staff and called, "Johnson, read Section 222 and 223 of the Regulations for everybody to hear. All of you close your mouths like say your papas and mamas born *una* without mouths but with eyes and ears. No small noise, okay?"

"Yes, sir," they answered.

"*Oga*, we *nogo* understand the big English *wey dey* that *una* mining law. *Na* small-small we *dey take* hear English. Some *no* hear *am patapata*," Uban Daba complained.

"Don't worry, those that hear small-small can explain to you" Sergeant Donald said.

Johnson went and stood upon a heap of soil by a loto hole at the centre of the people and began to read. When those that could reasonably understand English heard of the benefits of the extensions services, they shouted in joy.

"Mudi, *menene sun fada* (what did they say)?" one man asked as he saw people laughing. Mudi could hear English a little for human relation. His explanation to him had so much bearing on Section 223(1)(b) which is the effect of Section 34(2)(d) of the Act which provides that artisanal and small scale operators can access the Solid Minerals Development fund.

"Johnson, open quickly to Section 91 of the Act for the details of the extension services. It will be good for them to hear this also," Engr. Sluice instructed.

'The Government through the Ministry shall provide the following extension services to duly registered and performing mining co-operatives of small scale and artisanal miners,' he began, *'....'* They were exceedingly joyful when they heard Sections 91(e), 91(f), 91(g) and 91(j) which have components of acquisitions of skills in mining, hiring of mining equipment, mineral processing technology skills and marketing their products respectively.

"Bulldozer, are you satisfied?" Engr. Sluice asked.

"Yes, sir, but I have another question."

"Ask; we are here to help you."

"Sir, how will the government help us market our minerals? When Johnson *dey* read *una* mining laws *e be say* I *hear am* mention marketing; *no be so?*" He asked his colleagues.

"*Na so*, Bulldo!" They responded.

"Yes, the government of this country knows how you are suffering but gaining a little. The Mineral Dealers smile to their bank accounts at your expense. They will sit in huts shielded from the heat of the sun and the dangers of collapsing roofs of lateral mining you are subjected to, as animals that live in holes, and give you just small amount of money because you have no access to local or international markets."

"Yes, sir! *Wannan shine maganar! Cigaba, Oga* (This is the case! Continue, *Oga*)," Mudi said.

"So, in Section 95 of the Act, the good government of this great country, Nigeria, pitied *una* and established Mineral Procurement Centres called Minerals Buying Centres for *'proceeds recovered under a small scale mining lease'* to help *una get* sure and accessible market to make good profit and the

23

government to collect its royalty to boost the economy of this country," he explained and once again asked Johnson to read Section 224 of the Regulations which prescribed the requirements for registration of a Mineral Buying Centre. One of the requirements as provided in Section 224(g) is that the applicant should have minerals testing equipment.

"But are they functioning?" Bulldozer asked.

"Mmmmm, yes; the government is doing her best to see that they start to operate. You know any new thing has some teething problems. The government is working hard on that. Be patient," he answered and shook his head in worry on how government's projects are normally abandoned and asked, "any other question?"

"Yes, sir," Buldozer said.

"*Na* only you have questions? Let other people ask," Sergeant Donald said.

"Correct, Sergeant," one informal miner who had just returned from an illegal mining camp in the Western Region of Ghana said and quickly moved forward and positioned himself strategically for all to see him.

"Sir, before I *comot* for this country *go* Ghana two years ago, I know *say* we small people have problem of getting a portion so that we fit get Licence. Anywhere we go we keep on hearing one thing and *wetin be* that thing? Always we hear *say* one big man or big company have Licence over the place and now you *dey* say we should get a place for ourselves. How *dis go dey* possible? Tell us, please," the man asked.

"Yes, my friend, the Mines Inspectorate Department has been reporting this to the Mining Cadastre Office and I think it is seriously considering how to handle this situation to help people like you

24

and to reduce illegal mining. I know our former Minister tried to find a solution to this by making the holders of Exploration Licences (EL) to see the need of carving out of their Exploration Licences few Cadastral Units (CUs) for people to take up Small Scale Mining Leases (SSMLs). In fact, it has worked in few instances. Just give the government more time to find adequate and legal solutions to this; okay?"

"Yes, sir; it is better because many of *dis* Exploration Licence sites *dey* lie there with no company *wey dey* work *dem*," the man said, looking unsatisfied.

"In fact, let me tell you that even some big companies who have the requisite working capital as demanded by Sections 54(1)(a) and 27 of the Act and the Regulations respectively to mine the minerals are equally experiencing similar problems because of these speculators. They find it difficult to get open areas to take up mining Licence. Don't worry; the government is already doing something about this. Just wait," Engr. Sluice continued.

"Who are speculators?" Mudi asked.

Engr. Sluice laughed and began to explain, "Speculators are those people who just covered areas with Licence without intention to mine the minerals. They get Licence for the areas and wait for both big indigenous and international mining companies to come and buy from them at high prices. This is not good for the country as real and serious investors in the sector are normally sent away to favourable mining destinations. The government is equally doing something about this."

"*Ego* be good for the government to do something quickly for us to have our Licence. This *wahala* (suffering) for us too *mach* (much)," Uban Daba who had been very attentive spoke.

"Yes, the *wahala* too much! We *don* tire. Chief *go* say *en* own, police *go* say *en* own, land owner *go* say *en* own, youths *go* say their own and the government *go* say *en* own. We *dey* share the small thing we *dey* get with all of them. *Wetin* we *go* do as we *no* get power?" a man grumbled.

"Don't worry." Engr. Sluice encouraged them and said; "though you are yet to have your own site, let me just tell you something about mining in a Small Scale Mining Lease (SSML)."

"Keep quiet and listen, gentlemen!" one of the illegal miners shouted.

"My friend," Engr. Sluice called the illegal miner who had just spoken, "you have done a good thing but you people are not gentlemen and why did I say so? Because you are disobeying the laws of the land by mining illegally and see how some of you have been making noise as I am addressing you. Gentlemen are honourable men who don't behave like this. Anyway, forget about that. Section 48 of the Regulations says that in a small scale mining there should not be extensive and continued use of explosives or extensive and continued use of toxic chemicals or agents. It also says that it should not use or employ more '*than 50 workers in a typical day and that there should not be underground working more than 7 meters below the surface of the ground or galleries extending more than 10 meters from a shaft.*'" He turned round, looking at the scattered loto holes, and said, "But you people have sunk holes of even more than 20 meters with extensive internal spreads without pillars as found in an informed Room-

and-Pillar mining method. That is why many of you have been dying from collapsing walls or roofs."

"Even one …," one illegal miner wanted to say something, interrupting him.

"*In ka fada za mu jiji maka* (if you say, we will deal with you)," Dogo warned. The person had wanted to say that even a month ago loose walls collapsed on two of them and killed them. They had decided to keep this as a secret.

"What did he want to say?" Engr. Sluice asked.

"Forget about him, sir. *Na yeye* person *im* be," Uban Daba said.

As they were talking, a group of armed bandits, many of them, emerged from the north of the surrounding bush.

ॐ

"Any attempt to try escaping, will be met with death! Bring out the gold you have gotten! Who is Uban Daba here?" the leader of the armed bandits spoke in a harsh voice.

"*Yalabe, ni ne* (Your honour, I am)," Uban Daba said, still lying face down and raising his hand.

"Stand up and bring your gold first and others should do likewise!"

"*Yalabe, e dey* with Corporal... I don't know his name; the gold, for all of us, *dey* with *tam*. The Inspector of the minerals asked us to give him," he said, pointing at the direction of the Corporals.

"If you are the Corporal with the gold, bring all the gold with you. Don't try to be smart. We are not ready to kill again. We have shed a lot of blood. But we will not hesitate to waste you if you prove stubborn." The Corporal in custody of the gold dust obeyed.

"Who is the Inspector here? Is it the Inspector of Police?"

"*Yalabe*, no be Inspector of Police but for minerals," Uban Daba quickly answered.

"I am the one, sir," Engr. Sluice said and indicated himself by a raised hand, regretting he had addressed a rogue as sir.

"Come here?" He went.

"What is it in this your pocket? Is it gold?"

"No; it is a GPS, sir," he answered.

"What do you mean by a GPS?"

"It means Global Positioning System."

"You are an Inspector of Mines. I am an Inspector of Pockets. Let me inspect your pockets to see whether there is gold. I know you will want me to say I am searching you. The word 'search' is not appropriate here for a reason known to me." He only found some money which he removed.

Other armed bandits sought the pockets of others and removed various sums of money.

"Gagara," the leader of the bandits called one of his members, "take away the guns of those police men though they are inferior to ours. The Police must be rendered harmless as we escape."

After some minutes, Engr. Sluice and the rest of the people stood up, still afraid. They were not sure whether the armed bandits were coming back. They had gone far.

೮೦೦೪

"Sergeant," Engr. Sluice called, "I am ashamed of you! You allowed these rogues to humiliate us! Why didn't you fire at them when they came? You people are women!"

"*Oga*, how many of us are here? You know the armed bandits are many and have more sophisticated guns than ours. We couldn't have withstood them even if we had confronted them. You know this; *haba*," Sergeant Donald responded, suppressing his anger.

"Uban Daba, did you connive with them to deal with us for you to later meet them for an agreed amount?" Engr. Sluice interrogated him.

"How you *go* say *dis* kind thing to me, sir? I don't know *wetin* you *dey* talk *o. Na* you *sabi wetin* you *dey* say," Uban Daba was furious.

"We have been hearing of such connivance between illegal miners and armed bandits who normally use illegal mining sites to charge their phones," Engr. Sluice kept on saying.

"I *no* know *wetin* you *dey* say, sir. *Make* you *no* make me mad as *dis* situation *no* good," Uban Daba said.

They were all quiet for a moment in sadness.

"I know what to do next time," Engr. Sluice broke the silence and asked them to go, warning the illegal miners to vacate the site for Messrs Mining for Nigeria Progress Plc to start her exploration works on the condition that she meet the minimum work obligations as stipulated in Section 43 of the Regulations. According to these Regulations, if the Mines Inspectorate Department is not satisfied with the level of compliance, it would notify the mighty Mining Cadastre Office for the revocation of the title in accordance with the provisions of Section 97 of the Regulations.

THREE

"Johnson," Engr. Sluice, the Inspector of Mines, called, sitting by the edge of a conference table in his office, considering a point in a topographical map of a scale of 1:50,000 as prescribed for cadastral maps in Regulation 107(2), using latitude and longitude readings. It was a point at a quarry face of a well-known company in civil works, Elephant Nig. Limited. Johnson had taken the co-ordinates of the point when he was recently sent to the quarry at Kurmin in Kano State. Johnson did not hear him. He was busy reading Sections 75 and 76 of the Act that discusses quarrying. In section 75, naturally occurring quarriable minerals such as china clay, marble and gypsum are listed.

"Johnson!" he called again loudly, pacing in his office, holding an engineering pencil. Johnson heard him this time; he closed the Act and rushed to him.

"Did you see Mr. James Pull, the Project Manager, the other time you went to their quarry in Kurmin?"

"No, sir; it was the Quarry Manager, James Hope, I saw."

"The youths leader, Khalifa Umar, of the community was here recently when you were away. He came with three other fellows to complain on blasting impacts on the community. They seem to have a point. The company has failed in the observance of its social obligations to the community. It is our duty to help this community to enjoy part of the social and economic benefits of this company as provided for in Section 116(1) of the Act which speaks on Community Development Agreement (CDA)," he said and bent over the map, searching for the point he had lightly marked with pencil.

"Yes, this point you took when you went there shows that the quarry face is close to, and is facing, the village. The impacts of blasting operations must be disturbing to the community. Johnson, tell me two impacts of blasting operations." He had recently lectured them on that and on blasting patterns.

"One is air-blast, and the second is lateral vibration which can lead to the cracking or the collapsing of buildings," Johnson answered confidently with joy.

"Yes, you are correct. The Kurmin community may be experiencing these whenever the company carries out blasting operations especially when a massive one is done."

"It is true, sir."

"The Zonal Co-ordinator for Mines Environmental Compliance (MEC) Department has gone to Cape Town, South Africa, with the Hon. Minister to attend this year's conference of African Mining Indaba. When he comes back, he must see to it that the company complies with the social concerns of the community as prescribed in Section 174 of the Regulations. They are exposed to health hazards due to fumes," he said, still bending over the map, encircling the rock the company was quarrying as outlined by its contours. "Johnson, this is a massive rock; the company will work there for many years. The company needs a massive rock outcrop like this one because the project it is doing is a dam of average dimensions of 8,000m by 5,000m by 20m."

"Yes, sir," Johnson responded and asked, "sir, what is this Indaba all about?"

"Mining Indaba is the largest annual mining event in Africa. It attracts participants across the spectrum of stakeholders in the mining industry such as international financial institutions, major and junior mining companies. It presents an enormous opportunity for people to know about developments in the African mining environment and to see how to keep moving it forward. It serves as a networking platform for stakeholders."

"That is a very important forum for miners to interconnect," Johnson said.

"It is; in this year's conference, our Minister will, among other things, explain how the Nigerian mining laws are attractive to investors. You know the vision of the Ministry is *'to transform Nigeria's solid minerals and metals sector into an irresistible destination of global capital, attracting foreign direct investment to grow the sector to optimum level.'* Can you tell me the Mission Statement of the Ministry?"

Johnson smiled because he had memorized it long time ago as he suspected that the Director of Mines could bring that up as a question in a promotion examination one day. "The Mission Statement of the Ministry is *'Exploitation of mineral endowments spread across the nation and the establishment of a vibrant metal industry for wealth creation, employment generation, poverty reduction, promotion of rural economy and significant contribution to the Gross Domestic Product of Nigeria,'*" he answered with happiness, hoping he would be asked that question one day in a promotion examination. Engr. Sluice was happy with him because he answered the question correctly.

The Secretary to the Inspector of Mines entered the office while they were discussing.

"Yes, what is it Alice," Engr. Sluice asked, leaving the conference table to his seat.

"You have some visitors, sir."

"From where?"

"I don't know, sir." It was James Pull and James Hope that came.

"Let them in," he said and began to arrange his table. The table had many files on it that required his attention. The previous day he was occupied with the National Security Adviser on the issue of the breach of Section 69 of the Explosives Regulations of 1967 by a company that had imported a great consignment of explosives into the country without having obtained an Import Permit. It was discovered that the company had no history of previous dealings with the Ministry of Mines and Steel Development on explosives. It was a notorious company known for nefarious activities in sub-Saharan Africa and suspected to have links with terrorist groups and to be in possession of enriched uranium.

"Mr. Pull, you're welcome. Both of you sit down, please. Nice having you at this very time," Engr. Sluice welcomed them.

"Thank you Inspector of Mines," James Pull, the Project Manager, said.

"Let me hear you, please," Engr. Sluice said and called Alice to come and switch on the air conditioning system in his office. The weather was so humid.

"The rains will soon be here again," James Hope remarked, saying the weather was showing some signs towards that. He was greatly worried about how they would battle with the draining of water from the quarry face. They had wrongly situated the quarry face against the dictates of the terrain of the area.

"Oh, yes, it seems so," Engr. Sluice agreed and said to them, "once again, you are welcome. Let me hear you, please."

"Inspector, I am here on the issue of our magazine at our Kurmin quarry. The Explosives Magazine was broken yesterday by unknown persons. In line with the provisions of Section 9(3) and Section 22(4) of the Explosives Regulations, I immediately reported the theft to the Police Station and I am here now to report that to you."

"In this volatile period of the history of this nation that suicide bombers are ravaging the whole country?" Engr. Sluice said and stood up from his swivel chair and said, "Mr. Pull, you have been warned to secure the explosives storage facilities in conformity with the new guidelines and you have failed to! You have also been advised to increase the number of anti-bomb squads guiding your storage facilities. Did you do that? Answer me!"

"Yes, I did. The thieves overpowered them, Inspector. However, they are under investigation right now at the Police Station."

"Are they suspects?"

"Not really. But normally they should be questioned, Inspector. Don't you think so?"

"Where is your Section 9(1) Manager? He was referring to Section 9(1) of the Explosives Regulations that provides for the employment of a responsible person as the Manager who shall at all times be in the immediate charge of the explosives as authorized in writing by an Inspector of Mines.

"We only have a Blaster."

"Oh, no, Mr. Pull, for how long shall we continue to tell you the relevance of Section 9(1) Manager concerning explosives matters? He is the right person to answer our questions in times like this. You must immediately employ one. For now, any operation in your quarry is suspended until you employ one by my written authorization."

"I will do so very soon, sir."

It is unfortunate that many companies think that Section 9(1) Manager is an employee of the government. Go and read the Section under reference and you will understand. He is entirely different from a shot firer, the Blaster. They have different functions."

"I see," Mr. Pull said.

"Yes, many companies wrongly believe that the holder of a Blasting Certificate as provided for in Section 45 of the Explosives Regulations can concurrently play the role of Section 9(1) Manager. That is very wrong and professionally dangerous. A holder of Blasting Certificate is only responsible to seeing to the observance of the Explosives Regulations during blasting operations. You have to get this right."

"I understand. Mr. Hope, you should have told me this long ago. All this while I thought the Blaster is the right person in regard to the role of the Section 9(1) person," Mr. Pull said.

"Sir, I have been telling you this but you always complained of lack of money to employ such a person. What can I say? You are the Management," Mr. Hope reacted.

"Gentlemen, this is not time for apportioning blames. Go and bring applications for that position in your quarry. Applicants must be Mining Engineers who technically know much about explosives and will be able to render monthly returns on explosives to the Inspector of Mines as provided for in Section 63(1)(a, b, c and d) of the Explosives Regulations. Such returns should reach the Inspector not later than the tenth day of the month subsequent to that which the returns refer as provided for in Section 63(2) of the Explosives Regulations. Mr. Pull, do you get me?"

"Yes, I do."

"That is good; go and comply immediately."

"Mr. Hope, you must press for this. Do you get me?" Mr. Pull said in an executive style.

"Yes, I do."

"Mr. Pull, the day after tomorrow we shall be in your quarry because of the theft of the explosives," Engr. Sluice said and called Alice.

"Alice, bring the drinks," and turned to Mr. Pull and Mr. Hope and said, "You might be thirsty."

"That is nice of you, Inspector. We do appreciate your hospitality," Mr. Pull commended.

Alice entered and offered them bottles of cold water and soft drinks.

"Go and stamp-receive this letter. Johnson knows which file this letter will be filed in," Engr. Sluice instructed Alice. He was referring to the letter of the report of the theft of the explosives brought by Mr. Pull.

"I know the file. It is right now on my table. You worked on it this morning," Alice said.

"Okay, file and bring it to me quickly."

"She seems to be a hard working Secretary, Inspector," Mr. Hope observed.

"She is and she knows her job. I am pleased with her," Engr. Sluice agreed.

"*Ehen*, Mr. Pull, the youths leader of Kurmin community and some youths came here some days ago. They complained about your lack of implementing social corporate responsibilities to the community. As provided for in Section 116(2) of the Act, the Community Development Agreement (CDA) is essentially '*undertakings with respect to the social and economic contributions*' a company '*will make to the sustainability of such community.*' The prescriptions on this Section 116 of the Act are in Section 185 of the Regulations."

"We are on it, sir. It is unfortunate that the youths are not giving us the chance to get over this. They are unreasonably harsh with us. After all, the project is for their benefit," Mr. Pull said, looking worried. The Community had demanded too much from the company and he was imagining how the company would meet the demands if she agreed.

"Don't say that, Mr. Pull. They are right. You have violated the provisions of Section 71(c) and 118(iii) of the Act and the Regulations respectively by not concluding the issue of Community Development Agreement (CDA) with the host community before commencing work. You begged this office to discretionally allow you to commence work while the discussion on it is on-going to enable you to deliver your project on schedule because it is of strategic importance to this nation. Based on this consideration, this office allowed you to commence the work. The community reported that you are reluctant to continue with the discussion on the CDA. Why would they not react? Let us be honest, Mr. Pull."

"We have been serious, Inspector. We just want to be careful to see that we discuss with the people that really matter, and to implore the community to reduce her demands on the company. We have been hearing of reported cases of failed CDA because of wrong persons that were involved," Mr. Pull explained.

"I understand you. Actually you need to be careful and make sure that you hold consultations with the host community when implementing the CDA as stipulated in Section 185(2) of the Regulations but you must be seen to be committed to this."

"I am now happy that you understand."

"I always do. You should also make sure that the signatories to the CDA are persons freely chosen by the generality of the community to represent them as prescribed by Section 185(6) of the Regulations, and that the head of the community, prior to the signing of the agreement, submits to the Ministry the full names and addresses of the representatives of the community. They should not be less than 3 or more than 7 as stated in Section 185(7) of the Regulations. Mr. Pull, this is very, very important as the list shall be verified by the Ministry through any of its relevant agencies or departments and in consultation with the State Mineral Resources and Environmental Management Committee (MIREMCO) and the Chairman of the concerned Local Government as Section 185(8) of the Regulations says.

"Inspector, is CDA applicable to all mineral titles?" Mr. Hope asked.

"That is an important question. The answer is categorically no. Section 118 (1)(iii) excludes Exploration Licence holder from entering into CDA. Of course, a holder of a Reconnaissance Permit is also exempted. In both cases, the investor is still searching for the minerals."

"I was told some communities have asked companies still carrying out exploration works to enter into CDA."

"That is very wrong. This can scare investors away from their areas. People should always report such cases to the Mines and Environmental Compliance (MEC) Department. Actually, this department is responsible for this. I will introduce you to that department later."

"That will be good," Mr. Pull said.

"Oh, yes! This is very important also," Engr. Sluice remembered. "If a company and the community cannot come to agreement on the CDA, the Minister will intervene as provided for in Section 185(ii) of the Regulations."

"That is a good provision, indeed," Mr. Pull said and asked, "Inspector, you mentioned State Mineral Resources and Environmental Management Committee. Can you tell me something about it?"

"Yes, I did mention that. It is abbreviated MIREMCO as I have mentioned earlier. Section 19(1) of the Act provides for this. It is very necessary for me to list the members of this committee as contained in Section 19(2) of the Act to show how the Federal Government has recognized and favoured States and Local Governments in matters of administration of mineral title applications and the mineral titles. They are:

a. *A representative of the Mines Environmental Compliance Department in the Ministry who shall be the Chairman of the Committee.*

b. *A representative of the Ministry responsible for land matters or mineral related matters in the State.*

c. *The Mines Officers responsible for the State.*

d. *A representative of the Ministry of Agriculture or Forestry in the State.*
e. *A representative of the Surveyor-General of the State.*
f. *A representative of the Local Government Council when matters affecting the said Local Government Area are being considered by the Committee.*
g. *A representative of the State Environmental Department or Agency.*
h. *A representative of the Federal Ministry of Environment in the State.*

"Among the functions of the committee as spelt out in Section 19(3)(a – i), is to '*advise the Minister on issues affecting returns of necessary reports affecting grant of mining titles*' and '*advise the Minister in resolving conflicts between stakeholders.*' In fact, the Chairmanship for this Committee has been delegated to influential indigenes of the States of the Federation. Six (6) of the eight (8) members of the Committee are from the State Government. That is 75% of the members are from the State. By this, no State will say it has been sidelined on issues of mineral titles administration by the Federal Government," Engr. Sluice explained.

"That is very fair, indeed," Mr. Pull remarked and picked his mobile phone to answer a call.

ഇരു

"Yes, go on. I am hearing you. Is that so serious like this? Tell the Chief Security Officer to rush and ask for the quick intervention of the police. Don't mess about with my instruction over there! Mr. Paul, do you get me?" Mr. Pull spoke through his mobile phone, looking worried and agitated. Mr. Paul was his Site Engineer. He turned to continue the discussion with Engr. Sluice.

℘℧

"What is it, Mr. Pull?" Engr. Sluice asked.

"The villagers have blocked the road to our quarry. They said we must build a hospital for them. I don't understand this outrageous demand. To build a thirty-bed hospital! No! The company has no such capacity to deliver on that for now," he said, pacing up and down in the office of the Inspector of Mines.

"That is very unfortunate," Engr. Sluice remarked and advised Mr. Pull to leave immediately to go and contain the situation.

"Yes, we must leave now. Mr. Hope, let us go," he said, picking up his briefcase.

"Until I come for the inspection of the explosives storage facilities," Engr. Sluice reminded him.

"Okay, you are always welcome," Mr. Pull responded and sighed heavily and said, "Managerial position is not a joke."

FOUR

Johnson was in his office reading about relinquishment of a mineral title as provided for in Section 157 of the Act and given effect by the following Sections of the Regulations: Section 41 (for Exploration Licence); Section 53 (for Small Scale Mining Lease); Section 63 (for Mining Lease); and Section 74 (for Quarry Lease). He was refreshing his memory on how mineral titles could be relinquished. He had not known before now that partial relinquishment of a mineral title does not warrant revocation of the title except when it is completely relinquished. Sections 41(6), 53(4), 63(4) and 74(4) of the Regulations prescribed for this. In partial relinquishment, the mineral title holder shall adjust the boundaries of the mineral title in compliance with the prescription of Regulations 106 and 107 based on the type of the mineral title. Johnson was happy to have refreshed his memory with this knowledge. He was ready to educate a Mining Lease title holder who was planning to relinquish ten cadastral units out of his Lease to avoid paying annual service fee and surface rent of an area that was not payable. While he was waiting for the Mining Lease title holder to come, Engr. Sluice, the Inspector of Mines, sent for him.

ഇരരു

"Johnson, *Oga* is calling you," Alice, the Secretary, said.

"I hope there is no problem, Alice," he said, standing up to go and hoping all is well.

"I don't know. Are you afraid? *Na* you *sabi* (It is you that know) if you have done something wrong."

"I have done nothing wrong."

"Okay, just come," Alice said, going back to her office and walking with dignity like an ancient princess. Unfortunately, she was from the *talakawa* (poor) class.

ಬಿಝ

"Johnson, sorry; I did not tell you before now that we will be going to the Quarry of Elephant Nig. Ltd at Kurmin this morning. We have to be there today to inspect their explosives facilities because of the theft of the explosives they reported on Tuesday," Engr. Suice said.

"Okay, sir. Our work is like that of soldiers. One must always be ready," Johnson responded and silently thanked God for working under Engr. Sluice because he knew the job and he was learning so much from him.

"Good boy, I am happy you know that," he said, patting Johnson at the back with a smile of admiration of him and said, "I have taken it upon myself to groom you in this work. You will be an asset to the Ministry."

"Thank you. Sir, remember to take the GPS with you," Johnson reminded him.

"Oh, yes. It is already in my bag. I just bought new batteries for it. I hate disappointment when I am doing serious work in the field," he said as he remembered a time the batteries of his GPS completely ran down when he was working for one General Krukag (rtd.).

"It is normally embarrassing, sir."

"No doubt about that. *Ehen*! Take with you the company Quarry Lease, Quarry Returns and Explosives Returns files. You should also take the company's Explosives Magazine and Detonator store files; this is very important," Engr. Sluice said.

As Engr. Russo Sluice, the Inspector of Mines, was getting set to move, Alice came in and informed him that somebody had come to see him.

"Let him come in quickly, you know I am about travelling now," he allowed, standing up by his seat, hanging his bag on his shoulder and holding a helmet in his hand. He did this to sensitize the person who had come to see him that time was not at his side at that moment. Some people would prolong business or official discussion with social or political issues during business hours at the expense of work delivery to the annoyance of others. Engr. Sluice was conscious of this and he was blunt in checking people on that.

"Yes, Mr. Stope Basalt, you are welcome. Let me hear you quickly, please. As you can see, I am already set for a long trip."

"Sir, I am here with returns on quarries and royalty payment," Mr. Basalt said, stretching the returns and the cheque on the royalty to him with a boyish smile that would soon vanish from his oval face. He thought Engr. Sluice would be happy but it wasn't going to be so to his surprise.

Engr. Sluice squeezed his face as he read through the returns and the cheque and lifted up his eyes, looked at Mr. Balt and said, "For how long will you people continue to cheat the government in royalty payment? Atlantic Construction Company does primary blasting three times in a month and we all know how the company consumed a lot of stone

44

aggregates in the Kasawa-Wewi Road project, a distance of 115km with many bridges to be constructed. I will not tolerate this."

"Sir, the company is trying. This figure is not a small amount of money," Mr. Basalt argued.

"Mr. Basalt, you know this is not the first time I am making this observation to you. If you argue again, you will annoy me the more."

"Sorry, sir," Mr. Basalt pleaded and asked, "Can I have the receipt for the royalty payment now?"

"Of course, you can. However, be informed that your company will be sanctioned in accordance with the prescription of Section 20(4, 5) of the Regulations because your case is a clean case of intentional manipulation of the volume of the stone aggregates to enable you underpay royalty to the government. This is fraud," he said and read Section 20(4) to Mr. Basalt's hearing.

"*'A mineral title holder who intentionally, falsely or fraudulently, or attempted to reduce the revenue due to Government shall pay a fine in a sum of between One Hundred Thousand to Two Hundred and Fifty Thousand Naira (₦250,000.00) and in addition be required to pay any unpaid royalties.*' Do you get this, Mr. Basalt?"

"It's alright, Inspector," Mr. Basalt responded.

"You have the Regulations in your office. If you go back, read Section 20(5) for yourself to further see how enormous is the company's offence in this regard," he said.

"Okay, Inspector."

"Alice!"

"Sir."

"Come and lead this man to the Accountant. Let him issue a receipt for this cheque to him. Take the company's quarries return file with you. Mr. Basalt, follow her. I don't have more time to waste further. Inform your Project Manager of my displeasure over the issue of underpayment of royalty. Anyway, I will write to the company on it," he said and dashed into the rest room to perform a nature call function.

ℰℭ

"Johnson, where is the driver?" Engr. Sluice asked when he came out of the convenience. Johnson looked for the driver.

"Jegede, *Oga* is looking for you, come quickly. Your mouth *no dey* tire of continuous eating. If you are not eating heavy food, it will be biscuit, groundnut etc. as if you have ulcer," Johnson said to the driver.

"Let me finish eating my breakfast. I don't care about what you are saying. Wait for me, please," Jegede said, eating fast.

"Why didn't you eat since? I have told you that we may be travelling."

"*Na* you be *Oga* that you will tell me that we will be travelling for me to be serious? Why didn't he tell me of the journey since yesterday? As he has family, so do I. I need to inform my family. Don't you think so, small boy?"

"*Na* who you *dey* call small boy? *Yeye* man. Go and tell him that by yourself. I don't want your *wahala*. Why you *no* retire since *sef*? Follow me," he said as he began to go.

"You go die soon. Stupid and *yeye* small boy," Jegede said while washing his hands. Johnson went back.

ℰℭ

"Where is the old man, the driver, Johnson?" Engr. Sluice asked, yelling at the top of his voice.

"See him coming, sir." Jegede came running.

"Start the vehicle and let us go to Elephant Nig. Ltd quarry at Kurmin," he ordered.

"*Oga*, you for tell me that we will be travelling today. You know I suppose to tell my wife and the children. *Na* for them I *dey* work; give me something to go and give them for evening food."

"I don't have money. What about your salary?"

"Salary! You know how much I *dey* collect. My salary *no dey* last up to two weeks. Today *be* the fourth week we received salary and you know that."

"Jegede, is it because I respect you as an old man that you are talking to me like this?"

"*Oga*, you know I respect you well-well but one thing be *say* if person *dey* corner, he should *speak am* or he *go* suffer. *Abi*? If you don't have money, you can give me the two hundred naira you collected from me yesterday and gave your wife which she gave to Junior to buy biscuit when he cried for it. *Abi* you *don* forget?"

Engr. Sluice remembered and said, "Foolish man, take your two hundred naira. I had thought to give you one thousand naira but now you are behaving stupidly. You are lucky your house is by the road side. When we get there, stop and give the money to your wife. Tell her to come to the road before we get there."

Jegede phoned his wife, saying, "Mama Sand, come now-now to the road to collect money for evening food. I *dey* carry *Oga* to Kurmin," he said and started the engine. He slowed down as they got closer to his house. His wife was already waiting for them.

47

"Thank you, sir," Mrs. Jegede thanked Engr. Sluice as he added five hundred naira to the two hundred naira her husband gave to her. Engr. Sluice's humanity always overshadowed his harshness towards Jegede. Jegede would not like to part ways with him because of this.

"*Oga*, one thing I like you *e be* say sometime you do consider the poor. You see, you just gave my wife money now. I know I *go* eat meat today in my house. *Chineke* will bless you. In fact, *Chineke* said he who gives to the poor, lends to Him. God will pay you back *yafun-yafun*."

"Funny man, concentrate on the steering. We have to be in Kurmin at the scheduled time," Engr. Sluice instructed.

"Johnson, as we go, if you see any mining or quarry site, alert me," Engr. Sluice said.

"Okay, sir."

"*Oga*, I go tell you if I see one," Jegede said and veered off the road while dodging a pot hole. Luckily enough, he was able to control the vehicle back to the road in good time because he was almost plunging into a stream that had big stones. At that section of the road, the stream almost runs parallel to it.

"I am giving you the last warning. Don't talk again until I ask you to. That is how you drivers kill people on the road. Why did you dodge this shallow pot hole? You should have slowed down," Engr. Sluice spoke.

"*Oga*, if I enter it *gwarap*, you go say I *be* rough-rough or *yama-yama* driver. *Na* so you *dey* say always. That is why I dodged *am*. Only say I *no* see *am* quick-quick."

"Shut up!"

"Sorry, sir; *Oga na Oga*. I *no go* talk again," he said and slapped his mouth, saying 'make *no* talk again.'

"That will be good for you," Johnson responded.

As they continued to move, they passed many farms where they saw people working. They got to a certain place and they saw many tippers going in and coming out through one road that led to a river.

"Johnson, I am sure these people are quarrying this sand illegally," Engr. Sluice said and waved to stop a green Hillux car coming out from the river.

"Are you from where those tippers are carrying the sand?" Engr. Sluice asked the man sitting beside the driver.

"Oh, yes! You want to buy sand? I am the owner of the sand because river Gubi passes through my farm," the man said not knowing that he was making a costly revelation.

"Alhaji, Alhaji!" Engr. Sluice exclaimed.

"*Oga*, any problem?" the man asked and told the driver to switch off the engine of the car.

"You are doing an illegal thing. Sand is a mineral and minerals are controlled by the Federal Government for the benefit of all the people of Nigeria. The fact that the river passes through your farm does not give you the ownership of the sand or any mineral there," Engr. Sluice said and showed to him copies of the Act and the Regulations, telling him that "these are the mining laws."

"Mining laws for sand which God bring? This is my ancestral farm. Nobody will stop me from collecting money from these people."

"If you want to keep on collecting the money, come to my office next week and I will tell you what

49

to do so as to legally collect the money," Engr. Sluice continued.

"Where is your office?"

"Here is my complimentary card. The office address and my mobile phone numbers are there. Call me a day before you come, please."

"Okay, I hope to come."

"You must come, Alhaji, or …?"

"Or what, officer? *Na* we get this country. Don't make mistake even your Minister *na* our boy. You no *sabi* anything," the man boasted and finally introduced himself as Alhaji Sule Mai Dankali. Engr. Sluice recalled that he had been hearing about him.

"I will be waiting for you," Engr. Sluice said with finality and asked the driver, Jegede, to drive on.

"The man seems to be a big man, sir," Johnson said.

"No person is above the law of the land. He must formalize his quarrying activities if he wants to continue with the sand quarrying. Just wait and see," Engr. Sluice assured. He was not afraid of vested interests as he knew the President of the country was very concerned about the development of the Solid Minerals sector of the economy. He would not allow any vested interest to sabotage the President's effort on this. They continued with the journey.

"*Oga*, see people are massively quarrying laterite over there. It is a dome of laterite! An excavator is even there," Johnson said.

"We are getting late. You will be asked to come here very soon to find out who is violating Section 76 of the Act by carrying out quarrying operation not in accordance with the provisions of the Act and the Regulations. People just think they can do what they like in this country," Engr. Sluice said, looking at the direction of the laterite deposit. He told Johnson that it looked similar to an insitu mass of laterite he saw in Zambia when he went there some years ago.

"See another small laterite quarry over there, sir," Johnson said again after they had gone a reasonable distance.

"Stop, Jegede. Let us find out who these illegal people are," Engr. Sluice ordered. They went to the burrow pit.

"Do you have a Licence to quarry the laterite?" Engr. Sluice asked the leader of the people who were quarrying the laterite.

"No, we are digging the laterite for our mosque and our homes," the leader answered.

"Johnson, let us go." As they were leaving them, Engr. Sluice referred Johnson to Section 99 of the Act which allows the local inhabitants of an area to extract sand, clay, laterite and stone for personal use in accordance with the local customs of the community of that area and subject to sub-section 2 of this Section which prohibits the use of explosives in this case. "You young ones must know the law so that you don't mess up," he concluded.

"You mean the local people can exploit such minerals for personal use even in areas covered by Mining Leases?" Johnson asked.

"Oh, yes, Johnson. Subsection 1 of Section 99 under reference says, '... *nothing in this chapter shall be deemed to apply in relation to the extraction of sand, clay, laterite and stone for personal use by the local inhabitants of an area in accordance with the local custom of the community of that area.* '"

Time was no more on their side. They had to be at Elephant Nig. Ltd in the next 25 minutes.

"Jegede, you will have to increase the speed for us to beat time. However, it must not get to a dangerous level. If you want to die, leave it until you are driving alone in the vehicle. Johnson, *no* be so?"

"*Na* so, *Oga*. What does he want again in this world? Let him go!"

"I *no go* go. *Na* young men like you *dey* die like chicken now because of hurry-hurry to get money. You people are in hurry for everything. Your *gagara* too much."

"It is okay like that, Jegede; concentrate, concentrate. Remember if you want to die, you are to die alone," Engr. Sluice said.

"You *Oga sef*, I *no* understand you, I *no go* die and leave you, *Oga*. *Na* me *go* drive you so *te* I retire."

"Just *dey* go, Jegede."

Jegede increased the speed, entering pot holes anyhow to the annoyance of Engr. Sluice.

"Jegede, you want to kill us?" Engr. Sluice asked.

"No, *Oga*. Kill you and live with whom? I can't drive young *Ogas* like Johnson because they *no* fit give me money. Their hands *na* gum. They are greedy," he said, knowing he intentionally entered the pot holes to stop Engr. Sluice from slumbering. That was how he had been doing to him especially when they were on a long journey in the night. He would think of how he would be driving and Engr. Sluice would be sleeping instead of keeping him company through occasional discussion.

"Just go. You talk too much," Johnson responded with no interest to discuss issues like this with him.

"*Kwub! Meh... meh... meh...,*" a goat was crying. It had been slightly hit by Jegede with the side of the vehicle."

"What nonsense is this? What is wrong with you, Jegede? I will sack you! You are lucky the goat did not die. Had it died, you will have had to pay for it. I told you to be careful!" Engr. Sluice reacted.

"Sorry, *Oga*. I did not see it."

"How would you have seen it when you are rough?"

They finally arrived at Elephant Nig. Ltd quarry site.

&)G&

"*kwen... kwen... kwen...*" Jegede sounded the horn of the car at the gate of the company yard.

A security man came out and asked, "Whom do you want to see?"

"Which kind thing *be dis*? You *no* know us again? How I go carry *oga*, the whole Inspector for Minerals, come here and you *dey* behave like *mumu*. Open gate, my friend," Jegede spoke, fuming.

"I am doing my work," the security guard softly said.

"Who *no dey* do en work?"

"Jegede, would you be quiet? Who asked you to be zealous in this manner," Engr. Sluice interrupted.

"*Oga*, thank you for your understanding; we work here by order. If I am not careful, the company will terminate my appointment. One month ago, the Chief Security Officer was sacked for one small mistake," the security guard said and asked Engr. Sluice to call Mr. Pull's mobile number to tell him he was around.

"Mr. Pull, I am at the gate."

"Let me speak to the gateman."

"Mr. Pull wants to speak to you."

"Allow him in without further delay," Mr. Pull ordered.

"He said you should go in," the security guard told Engr. Sluice and opened the gate for them, looking downcast because of Jegede's poor interpersonal relationship.

₧₨

"Welcome, Inspector; how was the journey?" Mr. Pull welcomed him while shutting down his laptop. He was browsing on types of quarrying equipment the company intended to import from Germany.

"It was exciting; discoveries here and there as we were coming," Engr. Sluice responded.

"Discoveries?"

"Yes, Mr. Pull; discoveries of illegal quarrying activities. The Ministry has a lot of work to do. We are short of technical staff. I hope the Government will soon do something about it."

"You must persistently request for that. Anyway, can we go to the Explosives Magazine now?"

"That is why we are here. Since you are yet to employ a Section 9(1) Manager, call your Blaster to go with us. Where is Mr. Hope, your Quarry Manager?"

"He will soon be with us. Yes, he is coming. I can hear his voice outside. Mary," Mr. Pull called his Secretary, "call Salisu for me." Salisu was the Blaster, or to be more technical, the shot firer. The company recently sent him for a course on explosives in Sweden to learn modern blasting techniques.

"Yes, Mr. Hope, Engr. Sluice is here. He has just asked of you," Mr. Pull said.

"You are highly welcome, Inspector," Mr. Hope said.

"Thank you. We must start going now. We are not spending the night here; time is fast going."

"Oh, yes, let us go right away," Mr. Pull said and stood up to go.

ഇൻൽ

The company crushing units were in full performance.

"Mr. Hope, you people are violating the provisions of Section 202 of the Regulations by not installing dust or fume extraction facilities or using water to suppress the dust. See how dust is all over the place. I must not see this next time I am here," Engr. Sluice observed and warned as they were going.

"As a matter of fact, we spray water after two-two days," Mr. Hope responded.

"It must be every time you are crushing."

ഇൻൽ

They reached the Explosives Magazine. Engr. Sluice inspected it while Johnson kept on taking notes for he would write a technical or inspection report on that. The thieves had broken through the wall to access the explosives.

"Did you say 1,000kg of gelatin and 500 pieces of electric detonators were stolen?" Engr. Sluice asked the Blaster.

"Yes, sir; before the theft, we had 5025kg of gelatin and 4,000 pieces of electric detonator. But

55

after the theft I counted and saw that we now have 4025kg of gelatin and 3,500 pieces of electric detonators."

"Where is your register for the receipt and issuance of explosives as provided for in sub-section 0 of Section 37 of the Explosives Regulations?" Engr. Sluice asked the Blaster so as to exercise the powers conferred on him by sub-section p of the same Section 37 which provides that he can examine the register.

"Here is it, sir."

He examined it and made some notes and said to Mr. Pull, "You must restructure your explosives storage facilities in compliance with the new guidelines to prevent this happening again. A letter outlining what you should do has been written to you. Follow the instructions there to restructure the storage facilities. This must be done without further delay."

"Sure, we will do that."

"Let me see your maximum-minimum thermometer as provided for in Section 34(e) of the Explosives Regulations. Don't tell me you don't have it."

"Come and see it here, sir," Mr. Hope said.

"That is good. Mr. Pull, we have to go and visit the Divisional Police Officer (DPO) when we leave here. Can you come with me?"

"Oh, yes. It is my pleasure."

৯০৫৪

When they got to the DPO's office, Engr. Sluice said, "I am Engr. Russo Sluice, the Inspector of Mines. I am here to solicit for your support in tracking down the thieves that broke into Elephant Nig. Ltd's Explosives storage facilities. I understand the company has reported the case to you."

"Yes, it has. We will, Inspector. We are already doing a good job on that. We have started getting leading information on that."

"That is very good. Keep my office posted on your progress on this, please," Engr. Sluice pleaded and said to the rest, "let us go." They left for the office of Mr. James Pull.

ഇൻ

"Mary, bring the drinks. I hope they are cold enough," Mr. Pull said.

"Yes, sir, they are."

"Mr. Pull, despite your shortcomings, I am happy with your observance of safety measures such as using copper based locks and keys as prescribed in sub-section 3 of Section 34 of the Explosives Regulations. You have many positive things to your favour in this regard."

"Thank you for that commendation, Inspector."

"Yes, it is very necessary to praise a company when it has done well. We are not out to witch-hunt any company or anybody," he said.

"Thank you."

"We have to leave now, Mr. Pull. Remember to bring the application for the Section 9(1) Manager as we discussed the day you were in our office," he said after taking the drinks.

"I will send it to your office very soon."

"Mr. Hope, see you next time," Engr. Sluice said and started moving out of the office.

"Safe journey, Inspector," Mr. Pull said after seeing them out of his office to their car. He hoped to meet the Inspector very soon.

FIVE

Engr. Russo Sluice had just returned to rest in his office from a three hour interactive meeting he, as the Inspector of Mines, held with stakeholders in the minerals industry under the theme '*Nigerian Mining Laws and Discontents in the Mines Fields*' when some foreigners came to see him. Alice, the Secretary came to inform him.

"Alice, what is it? You know how busy I have been today. I need to rest at least for an hour," Engr. Sluice said and sighed wearily.

"I know, sir. But some people have come to see you."

"Though Government's business should not suffer, one must manage stress so that he does not collapse," he said and asked her to let them in, stretching his body and yawning heavily as if that would relieve him from the whole stress in his body at an instant. The dangers of stress as he was recently taught in a seminar of high ranking government officials was still very fresh in his mind.

"You are welcome, gentlemen," Engr. Sluice said to the foreigners.

"Thank you. I am Mr. Winze Shaft; here you meet Mr. Timothy Raise and Engr. Ramp Hill. We are from Australia, the home of mining," the leader of the Australian team introduced himself and those with him, and smiled broadly as he knew that first impression is very important. He was an amiable personality with great intelligence and great ability for abstract reasoning.

"Australia? Yes, it is the home of mining. The mining industry all over the world knows this. You are highly welcome. I am Engr. Russo Sluice, an Inspector of Mines. What can I do for you? Ammmmm; yes, okay let me listen to you," he said after briefly and successfully searching for a souvenir in a drawer he had wanted to show to them. It was given to him by a friend who went to Australia some years ago.

"We are here on a research mission to find out whether it will be favourable for us to invest in the minerals industry of this country," Mr. Winze Shaft said.

"Sure! Nigeria is a compelling destination for investors in minerals. We have almost all known minerals and most of them at commercial reserves. Also, our mining laws are investor-friendly and have been constructed to meet international standards. Our policy thrust for the minerals industry is to create an enabling environment for the flight of investment funds into the country. I think I have a copy of our National Minerals and Metals Policy," he said, searching for it on the table. "Yes, here is it; you can have it for yourself. It has a lot of rich information for investors in the minerals industry," he said and handed it to Mr. Shaft.

"I see," Mr. Shaft responded and thanked him.

"Yes, we have the minerals *yafun-yafun* all over the country," he said as if the Australians were Nigerians who would understand him.

"What do you mean by *yafun-yafun*, Inspector?" Mr. Shaft asked.

"It means in abundance."

"Good. That is the delight of investors."

"Yes, there are many minerals in abundance all over the country. A data base on that is being updated. The Nigeria Geological Survey Agency

(NGSA) is being empowered to do that," he spoke as if he was trying to block any loop hole of doubt from the minds of the Australians. He must, in his own little way as an Inspector of Mines, help the Minister who is so passionate to attract the mining majors into the country to promote the development of the mineral sector of the economy, to woo investors like these ones.

"I am impressed, Inspector," Mr. Shaft said.

"Our Mining laws provide good incentives for investors in the minerals industry; very generous incentives, especially for foreign investors," Engr. Sluice continued.

"What kind of incentives, Inspector?" Mr. Shaft asked, adjusting his position so that he could listen very well.

Engineer Sluice gave a copy of the Act to Mr. Shaft, and held another copy in his hand and said, "Mr. Shaft, open to Sections 23-28 of the Act. Here we have the fiscal regime on mining incentives for companies or enterprises. Are you there?" he asked, having opened to the Sections.

"I am," he answered.

"Some of the incentives as you can see are the deduction by a company *'from its assessable profits a capital allowance of ninety-five percent of Qualifying Capital Expenditure incurred in the year...of all certified exploration, development and processing expenditure including feasibility study and sample assaying costs and,'* of *'all infrastructure costs incurred regardless of ownership and replacement.'* Go to Section 28. Here is a provision for tax relief for a period of three years for a mining company with a mineral title, starting from the date of commencing the operation.

"It is very interesting to note," he continued, "that the tax relief period can be extended for a further period of two years subject to the Minister's satisfaction on '...*the rate of expansion, standard of efficiency, and level of development of the company in mineral operations for which the mineral title was granted; and the training and development of Nigerian personnel in the operation of the mineral concerned.*' Read the whole of Section 28. Is there anybody on this earth that will say the Nigerian government has not done enough in terms of incentives for mineral investors? I don't think there is one person," Engr. Sluice concluded and turned to Engr. Ramp Hill. "Engr. Hill, are these not great incentives for investors in the mining industries?" he asked.

"Inspector, they are but the reserves must be technically established to determine their viability. You know the industry is capital intensive especially at the exploration and developmental stages. As a Mining Engineer, you know what I mean," Engr. Hill responded.

"I have just mentioned that the Nigerian Geological Survey Agency (NGSA) is presently working hard on this. We have seasoned Geologists most of whom are members of the Council for Mining Engineers and Geoscientists (COMEG), the highest registered professional body for the earth scientists in Nigeria," he said with a sense of fulfillment because he was already a Fellow in the Council. "Mr. Shaft, Section 26 and 139 of the Regulations prescribed that mineral title holders must employ Mining Engineers or Geologists as the case may be, who are members of COMEG as Managers. It is good for you to note this as your company will have to comply with this to ensure adequate professionalism in your mining practice if you finally decide to invest in the mining industry here."

"Engr. Sluice, I am interested to know more about the Nigerian Geological Survey Agency; you know if we finally agree to invest in the minerals industry of this country we will have to interact with it," Engr. Hill said.

"The NGSA is an organization that performs one of the delegated functions of the Minister which Section 4(k) of the Act stipulates. He quickly opened to it and read thus; '*subject to the provisions of the Act, the Minister shall... develop a geo-scientific databank, and collate detailed data concerning the identity, quantity and quality of Nigeria's Mineral Resources...*' Read the whole Section to know the functions of the Minister."

"Does the NGSA have a mineral laboratory to give us the luxury of analyzing or assaying our minerals here without going through the rigour of taking them overseas?" Engr. Hill continued to ask.

Engr. Sluice laughed lightly, thinking that Engr. Hill was underrating the NGSA in terms of scientific facilities and said with a mixture of pride and joy, "NGSA has a unit, the National Geosciences Research Laboratories, which generates, collates, archives and disseminates geosciences data and information."

"I am happy to hear that!" Engr. Hill said, looking surprised and wondered why he was wrongly told before he left his country that he would hardly find a mineral laboratory in Nigeria of international standard. He revealed this to Engr. Sluice.

"I don't know why the International Community continues to underrate us. The world is now a global village and we are moving with international standards in everything we do day by day. We can't afford to lag behind. You people must know this," Engr. Sluice said, his voice choked up with suppressed anger and the fold ups in his face deformed it like a landscape deformed with folds and fault lines by seismic forces.

"We know you people are trying," Mr. Timothy Raise spoke for the first time. He seemed to be a melancholy with a scientific mind. Unfortunately, to the loss of the scientific world, he had read the Arts with passion because he knew passion is the driving force for any worthwhile achievement. He had no regrets at all reading the Arts.

"But the Western World is having difficulty in understanding us."

"We are getting to understanding you people. We will go back with a different and favourable story of your struggles," Mr. Raise continued.

"Do you know that the National Geosciences Research Laboratories based in Kaduna has the following equipment?" Engr. Sluice asked and opened to p.5 of a brochure on a brief history of the National Geosciences Research Centre. "See the function of each of the equipment next to its name in each row." The list of the equipment is as shown below.

NATIONAL GEOSCIENCES RESEARCH LABORATORIES AVAILABLE EQUIPMENT AND THEIR FUNCTIONS

S/N	EQUIPMENT	FUNCTIONS
1	X-ray difractometer (Empyrean)	Mineralogical Analysis
	X-ray Fluorescence	Elemental analysis

2	Spectrometer (Epsilon 5)	including major, minor and trace elements
3	Scanning Electrons Microscope (SEM)	Image analysis of rock samples
4	Eagon 2 (Automated Fuse bead maker)	Making fuse beads
5	Fume cupboards	Extracting fumes
6	Mini water laboratory 2800	Water analysis
7	Geiger counter	Monitoring radioactive elements in samples
8	Pulverisers	Sample preparation
9	Thermogravometricana-lyser	Carbon, sulphur determination
10	Thermoscientific Atomic Ansorption Spectrometer (AAS)	Trace elements analysis
11.	Milipal 4-EDXRF	Major, trace and rare earth elements analysis
12.	Perkins Elmer UV/Visible Spectrometer	For cations/anions determination
13.	Perkin Elmer Gas Chromatography machine (GC)	Organic geochemistry
14.	Hanna Ion Specific water photometer	Water analysis
15.	Firstch Pulveriser	Sample pulverisation

16.	Jaw crushers	Sample preparation
17.	Microscopes	Petrographic studies
18.	Petro Cut	Thin section preparation
19.	Petro Thin	Thin section preparation
20.	Petro Lab	Thin section preparation
21	Carbolite Furnace	Heating source
22.	Gallen Kamp Oven	For drying of samples
23.	Sand bath	For heating
24.	Hot Plate	For heating
25.	EM Separator	For separating magnetic minerals

Source: *Brief History, National Geosciences Research Laboratories, p.5*

Mr. Raise asked Engr. Hill to go through the list of the equipment for obvious reasons.

"This is fantastic, Inspector. We will patronize it should we finally decide to invest here," Engr. Hill said and handed back the brochure to him.

"When was this brochure written?" Engr. Hill asked.

"It was recently written and presented during a One-Day Workshop On: THE NGSA LABORATORIES, KADUNA: SERVICES, CERTIFICATION AND RELEVANCE TO MINING

AND TRADE on 19th June, 2014… at National Geosciences Research Laboratories…, Kaduna."

"I see," Mr. Ramp responded.

"You may wish to read Section 160 of the Act to know about geological studies and mapping '*for the purpose of determination of the characteristics and understanding of an inventory of minerals occurrences,*'" Engr. Sluice said, not wanting to continue with the discussion from the geological perspective.

Mr. Shaft thought for a moment, fixing his eyes on the ceiling as if he was admiring its modern design but he was thinking about something. Suddenly, he turned to Engr. Sluice and asked, "Inspector, can you briefly tell us the processes one has to go through in order to have a mineral title?"

"Of course; I am here to guide people on how to get into the mining industry. It is part of my work schedule," Engr. Sluice said with a professorial air of confidence. He had equipped himself with many of the critical mining laws by memorizing them. He was always ready to enlighten people at any given time. In fact, people referred to him as the 'Mining Law' because of this.

"Yes, I am listening, Inspector," Mr. Shaft said, shifting his chair closer to Engr. Sluice's table as if he had not been able to hear him very well. Engr. Sluice later discovered that Mr. Shaft had a medical problem with one of the ears because of long exposure to noise pollution in an Australian mine. Safety measures in this regard in the mine were faulty at the time the ear was affected.

"We have different types of mineral titles. We have Reconnaissance Permit (RP), Exploration Licence (EL), Mining Lease (ML), Small Scale

Mining Lease (SSML), Quarry Lease (QL) and Water Use Permit (WUP). All these have their specific and common requirements. I will only dwell on the requirements for Exploration Licence. I will give you a copy of the Guidelines on Mineral Titles Application for all categories of mineral titles," he said and called Johnson, who was by then with Alice, sorting out some incoming mails, to come.

"Johnson!" he called. Johnson could not hear him.

"Let me call him," Engr. Hill volunteered and stood up and opened the door to Alice's office.

"Who is Johnson here? Engr. Sluice wants to see him."

Johnson quickly responded

"Johnson, do we still have copies of the Guidelines on Mineral Titles Application?"

"Yes, sir, we have."

"Go and bring one copy immediately," he ordered and coughed to clear his voice and began to speak. "Before the boy comes back," he said to Mr. Shaft and others, "the requirements for Exploration Licence application are categorized into two groups and are as follows:

a. **Pre-grant conditions.**
  - Duly completed application forms.
  - Minimum Work Programme (detailed with COMEG stamp and signature).
  - Evidence of financial capability (Section 54 of the NMMA) with sufficient working capital by way of;
  1. Verifiable Bank Statement of account.
  2. Verifiable reference letter."

"Sufficient working capital is not a problem to our great company. We are already into the oil and gas business with huge financial capacity for diversification into many spheres of businesses. Like the eagle, our company has soared high and nested its finance on the financial mountain against any financial storm contagion," Mr. Raise interrupted, sounding as Grand Commander of the Financial World (GCFW).

"What is NMMA, Engr. Sluice?" Engr. Hill asked.

"It is an abbreviation for Nigerian Minerals and Mining Act. Please, allow me to finish telling you the conditions for obtaining Exploration Licence before you ask questions. Don't interrupt me again until I am done. That will be good for all of us," he advised.

"Yes, that is alright," Mr. Shaft agreed.

- "The remaining conditions are:
- CV and certificates of a Mining Engineer or Geoscientist registered with COMEG.
- Attestation of non-conviction of criminal offences under the Act.
- Evidence of payment of processing fees.
- Certified True Copy of Certificate of Incorporation including Forms CAC2 and CAC7, articles and Memorandum of the Association.
- Extant Tax Clearance Certificate for three (3) years.
- Irrevocable consent from land owners(s)/land occupier(s) with sworn affidavit in support of the consent by the applicant from a competent court, attesting that the consent was duly obtained from the land owners(s)/land occupier(s), Section 100 of the NMMA and,

-   Indication of minerals to be explored as required by Section 64 of the NMMA, 2007."

As he was concluding, Johnson entered with a copy of the Guidelines on Mineral Titles Application.

"That is good, Johnson. Mr. Shaft, here is the copy of…. You have it for yourself. Everything is there. Sorry! I have not told you the second category of the conditions for the Exploration Licence. They are called **pre-development** or **post grant** conditions. They are:

-   Reports from state bodies/MIREMCO.
-   Compensation.
-   Environmental Impact Assessment (EIA) in compliance with Section 119 of NMMA, 2007 and,
-   Closure plan/rehabilitation plan.

"For now, those are the conditions for obtaining Exploration Licence, pending future reviews." He told Johnson to go. "Mr. Shaft, it seems you want to say something. I am listening, please."

"I had wanted to ask what COMEG stands for but I remembered you had initially told us that it is the Council for Mining Engineers and Geoscientists."

"You are very correct. Remember its importance in the Mining industry of this country," he said. He hoped to be its President one day so as to move it to greater heights in all ramifications especially in professionalism and in the sphere of its influence within government circles.

Hung on the world to the right hand side of Engr. Sluice as he sat on his table is a composite geological and mineral map of Nigeria. Engr. Hill's attention was drawn to it.

"Inspector," Engr. Hill called, moving to the map, "can you and I have a look at this map?"

"Oh, yes! I was actually thinking of showing the map to you." All of them moved to the map.

"Engr. Hill, this is the gold belt that stretches from Niger Republic into the Northwest of Nigeria, passing through Katsina State, Zamfara State, then slightly through the southern part of Sokoto State, Kebbi State and down to the Southwest of Nigeria. Mr. Raise, gold is enough to give a progressive shock to the Nigerian economy. The present government is working hard to revive the minerals sector of the economy. The heart of President Muhammadu Buhari is there," Engr. Sluice said.

"Lead and Zinc is found here," Engr. Hill said, touching the spot with his index finger.

"Yes, that is in Wase area of Plateau State. Tongyi Allied Mining Ltd, which is, according to its table calendar of 2016, *living in mining heritage, developing World's mineral prospects* and aiming at *mining at a deeper level*, and other mining companies are committed to developing the Lead/Zinc mine there. You may wish to be there one day," Engr. Sluice said and turned to Mr. Raise. "Mr. Raise, you and Mr. Shaft are only comfortable with financial language. Ours is scientific and engineering language."

"We finance your projects. You engineers will have to lower your voices when it comes to issue of money. We determine what project to finance. I hope you believe that, Inspector," he said and laughed loudly as if he had caught Engr. Sluice in a web.

"I do but not always. The financial world is not only controlled by you people; the Engineers also do. How can you make your money in most cases without engineering inputs? Here, you are finished" they all laughed, patting one another on the back. Mr. Shaft finally said as they moved away from the map to their seats, "we all depend on one another to succeed."

"*Ehen*, Mr. Shaft, there is one very important incentive for mineral investors that I have not drawn your attention to. It is on custom and import duties," Engr. Sluice remembered.

"That is very interesting. Let us listen to you, please," Mr. Shaft responded.

"Section 25(i)(a) of the Act provides for the '*exemption from payment of customs and import duties in respect of plant, machinery, equipment and accessories imported specifically and exclusively for mining operations.*' Section 25(i)(c) also states that transfer of external currency of personnel remittance quota for expatriate personnel out of Nigeria is free from any imposed tax."

"The Nigerian government is really out to woo foreign investors," Mr. Raise said, picking a piece of sapphire on Engr. Sluice's table to look at. One miner had brought it to him as a sample without revealing its source. He had told Engr. Sluice to contact him if an interested investor appeared. He promised to take the investor to the site at a cost.

"Are you into the gems also?" Engr. Sluice asked Mr. Raise.

'No, we are for the metals and the industrials but mostly on the precious metals," he answered.

"However, Mr. Shaft, the Mines Inspectorate Department must approve the machinery, the equipment and the accessories to be imported by the mineral title holders as provided for in Section 25(2) of the Act. This is to check the abuse of this magnanimous policy."

"We understand."

"Yes, expatriate quota and residence permit in respect of approved expatriate personnel as provided for in Section 25(i)(b) is another incentive to foreign investors in the mineral sector. But ...," he was interrupted by Alice who came and told him that one man had come to see him.

"Mr. Shaft, somebody has come to see me. Let me briefly attend to him since we still have a lot to discuss."

"Please, do," he agreed, adjusting a gold ring on his finger.

The man came in. He looked gracious and composed.

ഇറ

"What is your problem?" Engr. Sluice asked the man.

"*Oga*, greetings first," the man said.

"Okay, you are welcome. How are you?"

"I am fine, sir, and you?"

"I am good. So let me hear you. I have serious people with me as you can see."

"*Na wa, Oga.* Is it because they are white people? Our company is also a serious company. You just *dey* do like *say* you *no* know me again. No problem."

"What is your problem, my friend?"

"Who *be* your friend? See the way you *dey* talk to me because *oyimbo dey* your office. No problem."

"Who you *be sef*? I can't remember who you are."

"Nnnnn, you *no* know me again? Today you *no* know Adit from Cool Exploration and Mining Plc.?"

"Oh, Adit, I remember! You know I saw you once and that day you were in your mining outfit. Today you appeared as a .... I don't know how to qualify you *sef*. So, what is your problem?"

"My *Oga* sent me to come and report that we have lost our mineral title and to seek your advice on how to go about it?"

"Tell him to apply to the Mining Cadastre Office for a replacement as provided for in Section 29 of the Regulations. When did it get lost?"

"It was yesterday."

"You must apply for its replacement not later than 7 days from yesterday in accordance with the provisions of Section 29(2). Two of the conditions for the certificate to be replaced are that you must obtain a police report and publish about the loss of the certificate in a national paper."

"Okay, sir," Adit said and asked, "these people are from which country?"

"Just *dey* go; what concerns you about them?"

"Bye-bye," Adit said and left.

"Okay," Engr. Sluice responded and turned his attention to Mr. Shaft.

ℴ)∞

"*Ehen*, now the man is gone. Let us continue from where we stopped."

"But what? You were about saying something when you were interrupted," Mr. Shaft recalled.

"Oh, yes, I remember. But the company's employment mix (Nigerians to Foreigners) must be favourable to Nigerians in terms of job opportunity and wealth creation. There must be adequate transfer of knowledge and skills to the Nigerians especially those understudying them to eventually take over from them. So in your application for Business Permit and Establishment of Expatriate Quota you must consider this."

"What are the requirements for the application of Expatriate Quota," Engr. Hill asked.

"They are as follows:
- The number of personnel and specializations required by the company.
- The Curriculum Vitae and Credentials of the personnel required by the company.
- The work schedules of the personnel.

"The applied Expatriate Quota positions should not include those that can be sourced locally. The Nigerian government will not tolerate this," he said.

"Inspector, my colleagues, and I have already formed an opinion about you. You are a nice person to be with. We really appreciate the attention you have given to us. We will like to go back to the hotel to have some rest and think of where next to visit. Keep on having a good day," Mr. Shaft said.

"It is my pleasure. Let me see you off."

"That is nice of you."

"*Ehen*, Mr. Shaft, you may wish to go and see the Head of Unit, Minerals and Metals Promotion Center in our Ministry Headquarters located at 1, Luanda Crescent, Wuse-II, Abuja. You will be further guided there. You may even request to see the

74

Minister," Engr. Sluice remembered. He advised them to go and see the Minister, forgetting that the Minister had gone to Tiangi to attend China Mining Congress Exhibition.

"We don't intend to see the Minister in this preliminary trip. We will seek for his audience through our Embassy when next we are here. We will definitely meet with him if we are finally convinced to invest here."

"I hope you will," he said and later returned to his office to arrange for routine inspection of some of the mining companies as provided for the Mines Inspectorate Department in Section 122 of the Regulations. In discharging its supervisory functions, one of its roles is to ensure that mineral title holders comply with minimum work obligations that may be imposed on them by the Ministry from time to time in pursuant to Section 122(1)(c) of the Regulations.

SIX

It was in the early hours of the morning of a Friday that Engr. Russo Sluice, the Inspector of Mines, finally decided that he would go to Messrs Minerals Economic Nig. Ltd on a routine inspection. The company was mining tantalite ore of a grade of 60%. She processes the tantalite ore at the site into concentrates. With this in mind, he went to the office that morning.

"Johnson, you will have to stay in the office today. Maxwell will go with me for the routine inspection. When Tanimu comes later in the day, attend to him on the issue of the half yearly reports. Refer him to Section 138 of the Regulations on this. Call Maxwell quickly for me," Engr. Sluice said and sank into his black swivel seat, relaxing as if he was no more interested in going for the routine inspection that day.

"Alice, must I remind you of the cup of tea every now and then? You should not be careless about this again," Engr. Sluice spoke, his voice was coarse as if he had been singing for a long time or shouting loudly in anxiety and fear.

"Sir, the milk has finished," Alice responded, with heart in her mouth in fear of the reaction of Engr. Sluice. She had been warned severally not to allow the milk to finish before she told him.

"Don't say that to me! Are you stupid? Why didn't you tell me this yesterday?"

"Sorry, sir," Alice said, almost stooping down as if that would neutralize Engr. Sluice's anger.

"Get out of here! When you get married and you allow food in the house to finish before you tell your husband, you will be calling for trouble into your marriage. Do you think I have money *yafun-yafun* to give you at any given time to go and buy the materials? I say get out from here!"

As Engr. Sluice was speaking to Alice, Maxwell walked in.

"Alice, why did you annoy *Oga* again? You this girl; I can't understand why you are very stubborn." Maxwell said with the aim to please Engr. Sluice.

"Don't look for my trouble, Maxwell. You know …"

"Did you not hear what I told you? You must get out of my office now!" Engr. Sluice fumed.

Alice went out and the day was not to be good for her anymore.

"Maxwell, you and I are going to Messrs Minerals Economic Nig. Ltd today for routine inspection," Engr. Sluice said.

"Okay, sir."

"Go and get set. We will be off in ten minutes," he said and began to tidy up for the trip.

80CG

"Alice, I came to see *Oga*," the Messenger in Engr. Sluice's office said. He was a man of unquestionable character and very loyal to the government by the way he worked. Engr. Sluice would always refer to him as the remnant of the colonial Civil Servants who were dedicated to the service of the nation, keeping aside vested interests and striving for honour like the lion among the animals in the jungle.

77

"Go and see him. *Oga* will always listen to you," Alice said as she knew how Engr. Sluice was so fond of him.

The messenger entered Sluice's office. "Good morning, *Oga*?"

"Good morning, my friend. How are you?"

"I am well, *Oga. Oga* ..."

"Yes. Say what you want to say quickly. As a matter of fact, I have only five minutes to spare for you," Engr. Sluice said, looking at the wall clock by his right hand side, ticking, *keg; keg; keg...* He would leave the office by 8:15am.

"*Oga*, how can a person export minerals?"

"You have come again. What is your problem with that?" Engr. Sluice said and wondered why the messenger wanted the information. The messenger had been asked to find out this information by Mr. Enoch Dayo, a business man who now found it difficult to access hard currencies, especially the dollar, to sustain his chain of businesses. He stays in the same neighborhood with the messenger and had known that the messenger worked with the Ministry of Mines and Steel Development. He had asked the messenger on how to export minerals so as to generate hard currencies.

"One man in my neighbourhood asked me to find out for him?"

"The man has a Licence to mine the minerals?"

"No, *Oga*. His, is just to carry different things to overseas to sell. *Na* big businessman. Even last year before the election, the Governor came to solicit for his support to win the election. He supported him with money well-well."

"No *be dat* one I want hear. You are a good person but sometimes you speak too much with salt in your speech. You have made me to speak to you like this … you know I respect you."

"You are my *Oga*. Even if you insult me, I *no go* revenge."

"Which minerals the man wants to export?"

"The man said industrial minerals like gold?"

"*Chai*! Gold *no bi* industrial mineral! It is a precious metal. Gypsum, kaolin, phosphate etc are the industrial minerals. Anyway, since the man has no licence to mine the mineral, he must start to comply with Section 133 of the Regulations which prescribed how to get Permit to Purchase and Possess Minerals. After this, he has to apply and obtain Permit to Export Minerals for commercial purpose in pursuant to Section 131 of the Regulations. But there are conditions attached to these."

"What are they, sir?"

"For the Licence to Purchase and Possess Minerals, the present conditions are:-

- Certificate of Incorporation
- Extant three (3) years Tax Clearance Certificate
- An attestation of non-conviction for criminal offences
- Banker's Guarantee as provided in Form 27 in schedule 3
- Source of supply
- Evidence of a technically competent person; and
- Payment of prescribed fee."

"*Oga*, all the laws *dey* your head; you really surprised me."

"Keep quiet and listen to the conditions for the Permit to Export Minerals for Commercial Purpose," he said but within him he was happy for the commendation.

i.   Certificate of Incorporation

ii.   Evidence of source of supply.

"Let me expatiate here. This source of supply is the mineral title from which the mineral is mined or purchased. The hard copy of the mineral title must be attached to the application.

"Sir...," the messenger wanted to say something.

"Just listen to me," Engr. Sluice stopped him and continued.

iii.   Reason for exportation or contractual agreement with a foreign buyer.

iv.   Evidence of registration with Nigerian Export Promotion Council.

v.   Extant three (3) years Tax Clearance Certificate of the company.

vi.   Evidence of the payment of royalties on the minerals to be exported.

vii.   Evidence of payment of processing fee.

viii.   Inspection report.

"One company paid the sum of Eight Million, Six Hundred and Seventy Thousand Naira (N8, 670, 000.00) as royalty to export 11.56 tons of tantalite concentrate last week. The same company paid Three Million, Seven Hundred and Fifty Thousand Naira (N3, 750, 000.00) to export crude tantalite to Britain two months ago. The present royalty rates for tantalite concentrate and crude tantalite are ₦750,000/ ton and ₦150,000/ton respectively."

"Apart from the royalty, is there any money to be paid to the government?" the messenger asked, wondering about the difference between tantalite concentrate and crude tantalite but he knew time was not on the side of Engr. Sluice to explain that to him. He later met Johnson on that.

"*Ehen*," Engr. Sluice said to the messenger, "if one mined the mineral to be exported from one's mineral title, one doesn't have to apply for a Licence to Purchase and Possess Minerals. One will just apply for the Export Permit straight away."

"Nnnnnn."

"Yes; oh, it is now 8.20! I must leave now. When the man is ready, bring him to the office to be properly guided."

"Thank you, sir," the messenger said and left while Engr. Sluice began to pick some items for the trip.

₮ℂℂ

"Alice!" Engr. Sluice called.

"Sir!"

"Call Maxwell for me!"

"Okay, sir!" she responded and rushed out. She ran into Maxwell, who was already coming to tell Engr. Sluice that they were getting late for the trip, at the door. Alice fell down. It had just rained early that morning. Mud spread all over her. She would have to go home immediately to change.

"Because *Oga* said you are travelling with him today, you just feel as if you are walking on top of the world. Your *garagara* is too much!" Alice said to Maxwell, fuming and surging towards Maxwell, raising her hand to slap him. Maxwell tactically dodged her. She missed him and slipped off her feet

81

and fell down again. This time, she fell into stagnant water. She was wet all over.

"Stupid man! Bush man!" She shouted and fetched the stagnant water with her hands and splashed it on Maxwell.

Engr. Sluice heard them quarrelling and came out.

"What has happened, Alice?" Engr. Sluice asked and silently likened the appearance of Alice to that of a miner who had just come out of a loto hole of poor ventilation in a high humidity tropical zone.

"Maxwell pushed me down," she said, almost crying.

"I didn't push her, sir. We collided. How can I intentionally do that to you, Alice? You must be fair to me! *Haba*, Alice," he said, touching his left shoulder which was paining him because of the collision. It was actually Alice that ran into him. He would have been the one to fall down if he had not been more balanced than she.

"You must quickly return home to change, Alice. Any wound?" Engr. Sluice spoke.

"No, sir."

"Sorry, Alice," Maxwell apologized.

"Don't say sorry to me. You are always colliding with people."

"How many people have I collided with, Alice?"

"It is okay. I don't want to hear any of you speak again," Engr. Sluice said.

"You, Maxwell, I know what to do with you," Alice said, pointing a finger at him.

"Alice, go back home and change," Engr. Sluice shouted at her and asked Maxwell to tell the driver to bring the vehicle for them to go for the routine inspection as he returns to his office.

ഇരു

"Sir, the driver is here," Maxwell said to Engr. Sluice.

"Okay, let us go."

ഇരു

As they were going, they came to a certain village and saw some people processing gold by the road side. Crushing machines were used to crush the gold bearing rocks excavated from a mineral title belonging to one miner called Mr. Lode Lapidary. He was a widely respected miner and known to Engr. Sluice for a long time.

"Jegede, stop; let me see who is doing this mineral processing here," Engr. Sluice told the driver. "Come with me, Maxwell." They went to the mineral processing shade.

"For whom are you working?" Engr. Sluice asked the people in the shade.

"For Mr. Lode Lapidary; see him coming over there," a supervisor told him. Mr. Lapidary was returning with the gold ore in a dump truck from the site.

"Oh, Inspector, you are welcome. I am just from the site. Oh, this hectic mineral business. It is not for women; you know. It is very stressful. But what can man do? All the riches of the world are buried in the ground. God wants man to work hard to earn a living. I think I am correct, Inspector," Mr. Lapidary said as if he was trying to make Engr. Sluice appreciate the efforts of miners - which he always does.

"Yes, you are correct; mining is for those who make hard circumstances their bread. You are one of them," Engr. Sluice responded, making Mr. Lapidary feel good. But he was a man that wore the robes of humility and perseverance.

"Thank you, Inspector; aaaaaaaa, I'm really tired."

"But Mr. Lapidary, why are you processing the gold outside the area of your Mining Lease. This is a violation of Section 135 of the Regulations which provides that a mineral title holder who processes minerals in an area not the subject of his mineral title must obtain a permit from the Mines Inspectorate Department subject to the submission of an approved Environmental Impact Assessment report and the processing plant design to the Mines Environmental Compliance Department and Mines Inspectorate Department respectively. By the way, this mineral processing shade is so close to the village. Have you not heard of the recent lead poisoning that claimed many lives in Zamfara State? We don't want a repeat of that in this country," he said and asked all the workers to stop the processing of the gold but they refused to obey.

"Can't you stop your crushing machines from working?" Engr. Sluice asked the crusher operators. He turned to Mr. Lapidary and said, "You must stop processing the gold here and relocate to the area of your Mining Lease. I am surprised that a person of your standing in the mineral industry can do this. It has been rumoured to me from a reliable source in Abuja that the Minister has choosen you to be part of next year's Nigerian delegation to Cape Town for the

Bi-National Commission (BNC) between the Republic of South Africa and the Federal Republic of Nigeria. If the Minister hears what you are doing here, he may reconsider making you to be part of the delegation."

In the following year's BNC, the Republic of South Africa and the Federal Republic of Nigeria would be discussing on how to co-operate in the fields of mining and geosciences. In addition, both countries would try to reach an agreement on a joint programme in airborne magnetic survey. The Nigerian delegation is hoping that South Africa would reconsider its local-foreign employment-mix-ratio policy in the context of African investors while the South African delegation is hoping to press for the waiver of visa for diplomatic and official passport holders. Mr. Lapidary would not like to miss this honourable privilege of being part of the Nigerian delegation to the BNC, and the Minister would not find it easy not to consider him as part of the delegation because Mr. Lapidary had retired as a career Diplomat into the mining industry. Therefore, he would be a double-edged sword at the BNC because besides helping the Nigerian delegation to strike a good bargain on purely mining matters, it is hoped he would advise it on the issue of repatriation deposits expected to be tabled for discussion by the Nigerian delegation. He thus has a master card in his hand and the Minister cannot afford to ignore him.

"Engr. Sluice, I can't process the gold in my Mining Lease area for fear of armed bandits. Didn't you hear of how 350 ounces of gold of 23 carat grade were seized from the mine of Ayi Azirki Dole Limited last month? Two persons were killed and many wounded." He turned and called one boy working at the shade, "Dankano, come here. Engr., can you see the wound in his hand? It was the armed bandits that wounded him when they attacked Ayi Azirki Dole Limited. Do you see why I said I will not process the gold at the site?"

Dankano was the person that ran away with Manir at Zumunci Mining Camp when Engr. Sluice and others went there. But how could Engr. Sluice know or suspect he was the one since he did not see him at that time? He is not the only person who bears the name Dankano.

"You will then have to comply with the prescriptions of Section 135 of the Regulations if you will not relocate to the area of your Mining Lease," Engr. Sluice insisted and asked him, "Have you submitted your application for the renewal of your Exploration Licence at Makogo to the Mining Cadastre Office as we spoke last time?"

"No, my Technical Manager travelled to South Africa for a month's course in one of the mines. When he comes back, he will do that."

"Mr. Lapidary, Section 38(1) of the Regulations says that renewal application for Exploration Licence should be submitted to the Mining Cadastre Office three (3) months to the expiry date."

"Yes, you told me that last time we spoke."

"Then why didn't you observe that? I still remember your Licence will expire on the 23rd of next month, less than two months from now. Now, one of the two things stated in Section 38(4) of the Regulations may well happen to you."

"Nnnnn...."

"Yes, the Director-General of the Mining Cadastre Office may either deny or consider the application subject to payment of non-refundable late filing fee specified in schedule 1."

"No problem, Engineer. You know I can pay the late filing fee," Mr. Lapidary said, waving the idea as a non-issue.

As they were talking, a group of youths from the village came, shouting. "Lapidary must stop processing his gold here! We are silently dying! He must leave this place! Many people are sick these days! Nothing was happening like this in our village before!" They were carrying cutlasses and sticks.

"What is it that is happening, Mr. Lapidary? Are we safe?" Engr. Sluice asked.

"Nothing will happen. They are hungry people. They don't know what they are doing. I will teach them a lesson," Mr. Lapidary boasted, knowing how dangerous the situation could escalate to.

"*Heh*, Saidu, stop that nonsense! You are the ring leader of this nonsense that is happening here," Mr. Lapidary spoke in annoyance. Saidu was the youths leader in the village.

"We cannot stop demanding that you leave this place. *Oga* Engineer, we learned that you are the Inspector for minerals matter. Many of our people are sick since this man started grinding the gold here. We don't want what happened in Zamfara State to happen here. But this man has refused to listen to us. Gargada, what are you people waiting for?" Gargada was the leader of the militant faction of the youths in the village. He was recruited into the Nigerian Police Force some years ago but he ran away because he preferred the natural set up of his village and its hinterland to the artificial environment and life of the city. Therefore, he would not tolerate anything that would disrupt the appealing serenity of the village and its environs, and that was exactly what Lapidary was doing.

Gargada and the rest of the youths started destroying the crushing machines and some equipment in the shade. A fight for all ensued with many wounded but there was no fatal casualty.

"Do you see what I was telling you? You must leave this place," Engr. Sluice said to Lapidary and intervened.

'Stop and listen to me! Stop and listen to me," Engr. Sluice shouted at the top of his voice.

"Gargada, control the boys," Saidu instructed.

"Everybody should retreat! Advance no more! Mission has been accomplished. Lapidary now knows our stance for him to leave this place is no longer a joke. If he still thinks otherwise, let him continue to process the gold here," Gargada said and calmed the boys.

"The Mining Manager will speak to us now," Saidu announced, referring to Engr. Sluice.

"My friends, I greet *una* all. Though what Lapidary is doing here is very wrong as it has to do with your health, I wish to clearly state that you have taken the law into your hands. Is it good that you have destroyed his machines and equipment? You should have complained to my office or to the police concerning the activities of Mr. Lapidary here. We know what to do. However, I assure you that he will relocate from here."

As they were talking, a contingent of policemen arrived in the scene, battled ready. One of the workers at the shade had called them when the youths arrived. Many of the youths were arrested to be interrogated. The wounded ones were carried to a local clinic for treatment.

"Mr. Lapidary, we are going now. I want to see you in my office next week, please. Remember you have to relocate from here," Engr. Sluice said and they continued with their journey. He wondered why Mr. Lapidary could not comply with the provisions of Section 162 of the Regulations by preventing the pollution of the environment.

჻჻

"Sir, what is carat?" Maxwell asked Engr. Sluice as they continued to go.

"Carat is a unit of purity in gold or a unit of measuring the mass of precious stones. Pure gold is 24 carat."

"Thank you, sir," Maxwell thanked him and hoped to know much about gold business so as to go into it when he retires from service.

"Sir, there was a time you asked one institution to give to our office a Certificate of Analysis on minerals samples exported for analysis. So there is something like that?"

"That is why you must always read the Act and the Regulations to equip yourself. Section 144 of the Act says for any mineral that is exported solely for analysis or experiment or as a scientific specimen, a Certificate of the result of analysis on the mineral must be obtained and delivered to the Minister within six (6) months of the export of the samples. Section 132 of the Regulations is also on export of mineral samples for analysis," he explained and wished the young Mines Officers would read the mining laws with passion to enhance work delivery.

"Sir, Mr. Oheli of Epicentre Enterprises Ltd was referring to quarrying activities as mining."

"What did you tell him on that?"

"I told him that they are two different things."

"Engr. Sluice laughed and referred him to Section 2(3) of the Regulations which says mining includes quarrying operations. "Maxwell, on a general term, you can say quarrying is also mining."

"Thank you, sir. I will begin to read the Act and the Regulations very well," Maxwell decided.

కాౖ

"Here we are at Messrs Mineral Economics Nig. Ltd," Engr. Sluice said as they approached the gate of the company.

"Is Mr. Benjamin, the Project Manager in?" Engr. Sluice asked the security guard, a slim and straight walking figure with protruding eyes. From his appearance and face, he seemed to be a chain smoker.

"Where are you from?" the security guard asked.

"Don't you know who we are?" Jegede interrupted.

"I have warned you not to speak when I am speaking. My friend, talk to me and don't mind him," Engr. Sluice said. "I am Engr. Sluice, the Inspector of Mines. We are from …," he was interrupted by the security guard.

"Oh, sorry, sir; you were here sometime ago! Sorry, I recognize you now. The Project Manager is on seat," he said and opened the gate for them.

కాౖ

"Sir, you have visitors," the Personal Secretary told the Project Manager.

"That may be the Inspector of Mines. I have been expecting him for some time. Let him in," the Project Manager said.

"You can go in, sir," the Secretary said.

"May abundant peace be unto this office," Engr. Sluice pronounced as he and Maxwell walked in.

"Inspector, you are welcome. What happened that you arrived behind schedule? I hope it is well."

"It is always one of those things, having to stop here and there as one notices some mining activities. Anyway, sorry for keeping you, waiting. How are you doing?"

"Fine, except that things are not as we earlier expected. We hope there will be improvement very soon. The fiscal regime is frightening. Anyway, nice to have you," he said, looking demoralized.

"Can we go to the mine now?" Engr. Sluice asked.

"Oh yes! You are here for that," the Project Manager said and told him that Engr. Elihud, the Mines Manager appointed in accordance with the provisions of Section 139 of the Regulations, was already waiting for them at the mine.

"Alright, let us be going," Engr. Sluice said. They left for the mine.

∾∿

"Engr. Elihud, how are you?" Engr. Sluice asked.

"Fine, Inspector. Let us go to the pit," he said and led the way.

"You have been developing this mine for the past two and half years. You will soon commence production."

"Why, Inspector?" Engr. Elihud asked. "We still have a lot of developmental work to do. It may take us another year to be able to start production."

"You have a copy of the Regulations with you. Regulation 118(2) says a mineral title holder should start mining operations in the title within 36 months of fulfillment of Section 118(1) of the Regulations which has to do with the submission of things like approved Environmental Impact Assessment statement, a detailed work programme, Community Development Agreement and a plan of mining operations in line with the provisions of Regulation 107(3), and you have done these things two and half years (30 months) ago. You must comply with the provisions of the Regulations."

"We hope to if funds are made available," Engr. Elihud said, hoping to hear the Project Manager speak but he did not say anything on that.

"Engr. Elihud, as Section 119(b) says, you must inform my office in writing within 30 days from the date you will start to produce the mineral."

"Sure! We told you when we commenced the mine development."

"Yes, you did well."

"Thank you."

"Regulation 119(c) says you will have to inform my office in writing of any significant change in capacity and stating the design of the mine within 30 days of such a change."

"We will do that if there will be something like that," the Project Manager said.

"Engr. Elihud, I hope you have read the obligations of a Mine Manager in Regulation 140. You must know your work so as not to be a victim of Section 139(c)(iii) of the Regulations. You know if you are not careful to guide your management as a professional, your appointment can be terminated," he said, not minding the presence of the Project Manager and the feelings of Elihud. One of the minuses of Engr. Sluice is that he has a low capital for empathy. He seemed not to be aware of this because he did not care. As they were talking, they saw some people approaching them, shouting.

"No, we cannot allow this! What compensation is he talking about? How can a foreigner stop us from farming our ancestral lands? We no *go gree lailai*," the people kept shouting. A man was leading them. They were coming from the nearby village to the site. "Let them bring the police to kill all of us today. Just small compensation they paid and they are denying us our means of livelihood. This must stop," the man said and turned and asked those following him, "or have you changed your stance on this?"

"No! We must farm in our land no matter what," the people answered.

From the village, an old man respected by the people rushed to the site to calm down the situation.

"Awolu," the old man called the person leading the demonstrators, "don't you have sense? Has not the chief told you that he was handling the case with the government? Though we need to farm in our lands, we equally need the company here. Is there anybody here who has not seen any progressive change in this community since the coming of this our friend? Yes, the company is our friend because it is investing heavily here and has told us that the village will enjoy social and economic benefits. Have we not started seeing this? Before now, we had to go to Garin Kwaranda, 40km from here, to have medical attention. Is that not so?"

"Yes, it is so, but…," the people answered.

"So, what are you telling me? Today we have a medical post to ourselves, built and equipped by this company who are yet to start enjoying the fruit of this massive investment. This village must behave well in appreciation for all this. *Haba, yara basu jin gargadi* (Oh, children do not listen to warning)," he said and turned to listen to Engr. Sluice who had been struggling to be allowed to speak.

"Can I speak now? Are you ready to listen to me?" Engr. Sluice asked.

"Continue, my friend," the old man said, not knowing that the youths were angry with him because they had learnt that the company was giving him money for times like this because of his influence. They were planning to ignore him.

"My friend, speak," the old man urged Engr. Sluice.

"I just have some few words for you people. You will have to go back and leave me to speak with the company on your behalf. You will farm in your lands but without interfering with the mining activities of the company. You may wish to note that Section 22(1) of the Act places the use of land for mining over other uses of the land and that Section 22(2) of the Act says that the Governor can revoke the right of occupancy, customary or statutory, within 60 days of grant of a mineral title to allow for mining activities but with regards to the provisions of Section 28 of the land use Act. So, take it easy. Go back as I have assured you that I will speak to the company. Thank you," he concluded. They went back with the old man. He would not stay back so as not to be suspected of connivance. Engr. Sluice was left with Mr. Benjamin and Engr. Elihud.

ഇരുത

"Mr. Benjamin, you will have to allow these people to farm on this land where it does not interfere with your mining activities," Engr. Sluice said.

"Why, Inspector?" Engr. Elihud asked.

"Yes, that is a good question." He opened to Section 101(3) of the Act and asked Engr. Elihud to read it aloud.

'Subject to the provisions of section(2) of this Act, the lawful occupier of any land within an area subject to a mining lease shall retain the right to graze livestock upon or cultivate the surface of the land in so far as the grazing or cultivation does not interfere with the mining operations in the area.'

"This is self-explanatory. Section (2) of the Act referred to is about *'prohibition of exploration or exploitation of minerals without authority.'* For now, I can see your mining activities are only within 1 cadastral unit (450m by 450m or 15" by 15"). Allow the villagers to graze and farm in the other cadastral units that you are not using now for the sake of peace."

"We will see to it," the Project Manager said.

"Engr. Elihud, you must strictly follow the pattern of your mine design as you progress in your development of the mine. We are going back now.

SEVEN

The previous night, Engr. Sluice, the increasingly becoming well known Inspector of Mines as a result of the on-going inspection tour of mines, received a call from the President of the Miners' Association of Nigeria, reminding him of a scheduled meeting.

"Inspector, I call to remind you of the meeting you and I fixed for tomorrow. I hope you have not forgotten. I am coming with my Secretary," the President of Miners' Association of Nigeria spoke, pacing around, at the other end. He wished it was a video call for him to see the Inspector live. It had been one of his pleasures to make video calls. He knew the Nigerian mining terrain so much and its discontents.

"Mr. President, I nearly forgot about the meeting. It has been a tasking period for me. Some of you miners are not operating in compliance with the provisions of the mining laws. Anyway, until you come tomorrow. President, what is the time we fixed for the meeting?"

"11:00 am."

"That is alright," he said, thinking of an appointment he had fixed for the same time with a Quarry Manager of a commercial quarry who had violated the Explosives Regulations of 1967. While in the office the following morning, he called the Quarry Manager to reschedule the appointment.

"Engr. Eugene," Engr. Sluice called the Quarry Manager, "I am sorry to inform you that our appointment scheduled for 11:00am has been rescheduled to 2pm. Sorry for any inconvenience that this unfortunate shift may cause you, please. Do you get me, Manager?" he asked and imagined how bad he would feel about it.

"No problem, Inspector; at your convenience, please," Engr. Eugene said but he was just being courteous for he had arranged to have a staff meeting at 2:30pm that day. He would have to shift it even beyond the next day as he has to accompany the Chairman of the company to a Federal High Court for a case the company had instituted against a man who had bought Three Million Naira (₦3,000,000.00) worth of stone aggregates of ½" and ¾" meshes months ago and had refused to pay the company at the agreed and graciously extended times.

"Thank you," Engr. Sluice said and turned to Alice, the Secretary, "Alice, do you know Alhaji Saminu Gogawa?"

"Yes, sir; I do."

"He will be here in five minutes. Allow him in immediately he arrives if I am not with anybody." He opened to Section 116 of the Regulations which is on the contents of minimum work obligations of mineral titles to vet the contents of a minimum work programme submitted by Across the World Mineral Exploration Plc, a foreign company. He was not satisfied with it. He decided he would advise the company to build another one commensurable to the approved machinery and equipment. He remembered the Minister had told the Mines Inspectorate Department to exercise its statutory function of prescribing the minimum annual work obligations of mineral titles as provided for in Section 116 of the Regulations. It had been effectively gossiped to the Minister that mineral title holders are toying with this very important issue of minimum work obligations.

"Alice!" Engr. Sluice called, "I saw Engr. Dayo coming in just now. Call him for me."

Engr. Dayo came.

"Engr., we have not been prescribing minimum work obligations for mineral title holders based on present realities. The Minister is not happy and has told the Department to do something about it. You are the Unit head for the minimum work obligations. I want you to draw up a draft of a review of the minimum work obligations on Exploration Licence. You have just returned from Australia. You must build a draft that will meet international standards. You know why I have put you in charge of that unit."

"As a matter of fact, sir, I have been thinking of this for quite some time," Engr. Dayo said, recalling how mineral operators in Australia are so organized. He remembered how Banksmen (authorized competent persons who supervise the lowering and raising of persons, materials or rocks in a mine as interpreted in Section 2(2) of the Regulations) there joyfully did their work with passion as they knew revenues from the mineral industry was critical to the budget position and the fiscal regime of that country. He relished on his experiences when he was there and said to Engr. Sluice, "*Oga*, the mining industry in this country still has a long way to contribute substantially to the Gross Domestic Product(GDP) of this country but we shall get there," he said with confidence because he hates discouragement and that is why his friends are only positive thinkers.

"Yes, Dayo, we will get there. The oil industry can no longer continue to sustain the economy of this country. Its market now is not as promising as in the past. Interest in renewable energy is now talked about all over the world. Anyway, go and build up the draft on review of the work obligations for Exploration Licence for now. Let me see the draft. Those of other mineral titles will follow later."

"Okay, sir," Dayo said and left. While he was going out, he saw Alhaji Saminu Gogawa in Alice's office.

"Alhaji, Alhaji! Are you still alive?" Dayo asked in a loud voice, handshaking him with a strong hold of his hand not knowing Alhaji Gogawa had a wound in the palm of his hand as a result of an accident in the mine in which one of his workers lost his thumb. The company, however, had chosen not to comply with the provisions of Section 130 of the Regulations one of which is to report about an accident in a mine to the Minister, the Mines Inspectorate Department in the State and the nearest Police Station within 24 hours of its occurrence. The company had not obeyed the instruction of the Inspector of Mines for it to strictly observe safety measures. She was afraid of being sanctioned if a report was made on the accident.

"Aaaaa, Engr, I have a wound," Alhaji Gogawa groaned but he would not tell him the cause of the wound.

"Sorry, Alhaji; you should have not given me your hand for the handshake," Engr. Dayo said and did not ask him of the cause of the wound and Alhaji Gogawa breathed a sigh of relief although he wouldn't have told him the truth of what happened.

"Alhaji, go in and see *Oga*. He has been waiting for you," Alice said, singing in a low tone a chorus which says poverty is no good and should be hated through hard work. She remembered it was recently stated in a lecture held in an agency auditorium that informal miners were contributing to reducing poverty in the land.

"Inspector, how are you?" Alhaji Gogawa greeted as he entered.

"I am doing fine, and you?"

"*Wallahi, sai godiya ga Allah.* Do you understand what I said?"

"Yes. I know Hausa small-small. What you said is that you are honestly grateful to God."

"Hahahaaaa, you *Dan* Ibo you *dey* try. We will give you one Hausa girl to marry as you can speak Hausa."

"Alhaji don't allow my wife to hear this from you. *Na* trouble you *go* bring for yourself if she hears you say this."

"Allah? She *go* give me *wahala*?"

"You *no* know? *Dey* there," he sighed and said, "let us leave the matter. What is your reason for coming to see me?"

'Inspector, you know my Mining Lease is for tantalite and columbite. In the process of mining the deposit, we discovered tourmaline. We want to mine the tourmaline. What can we do now?"

"Oh, Alhaji, you people have the mining laws but you don't read them. This is very unfortunate. This is a simple matter," Engr. Sluice said and moaned at the poor reading culture of the people.

"Inspector, what is your work? Is it not to read the laws and explain to us who have the money to invest? If *na* money, I can read it well-well. Nobody can confuse me on this," Alhaji said and removed a bundle of money and hit Engr. Sluice's table with it and said, "My language *na* language of money."

"Alhaji, Alhaji, to some extent you are correct because your Mines Manager is supposed to read and tell you about mining laws since you are paying him to work for you."

"*Ehen*, you understand now. How I *go dey* think about getting money and at the same time spoil my calculation with reading the mining laws?"

"Why didn't you come with him? I mean your Mines Manager."

"He is supervising the construction of an earth dam at the site."

"Alhaji, you are fond of coming here on purely technical matters without him. If I ask you a technical question now you will not be able to answer me. Next time you will have to come with him or just send him alone if it is not necessary for you to come. You don't understand the language of Engineers. You only understand the language of money as you have rightly said."

"Oh yes! The language of money is action. Right now my money is speaking the earth dam into existence," he said and laughed loudly, trying to shake Engr. Sluice but quickly stopped as he remembered the wound in his palm.

"Alhaji, your problem has been taken care by Section 88 of the Regulations. Since it is not a security mineral or a mineral water you can apply to the Mining Cadastre Office for the amendment of the Lease to include the newly discovered mineral which you are seeking authorization to mine. But you will have to notify the Mining Cadastre Office within 30 days of the discovery of the mineral as prescribed in subsection 1 of Regulation 88. However, the approval by the Director-General of the Mining Cadastre Office is subject to his satisfaction with your proposed programme for exploiting the newly discovered mineral."

"We discovered the tourmaline 22 days ago. We have little time left for us to notify the Mining Cadastre Office."

"Yes, that is the essence of having a good knowledge of the laws. Some of them are time bound. You are even fortunate that the 30 days have not elapsed."

"We will do that within three days. Inspector, we believe there is a large spread of the tourmaline in the remaining area of our Exploration Licence. We want to put in an application for another Mining Lease."

"There is no need for that. You can simply apply to the Mining Cadastre Office for the enlargement of the present Lease to cover the area of your interest as allowed by Section 64(1) of the Regulations. Your application will be granted except if Section 64(11) of the Regulations catches up with you."

"What does it say, Inspector?" Alhaji asked and took the bundle of the money he had boasted with and put it into his pocket. Engr. Sluice had shown no sign of interest in his money. He was a decent man.

"Your Mines Manager can tell you the details of that. But I don't think you will have any problem in getting your application through. You are a compliant mineral operator. I hope you have complied with my instruction concerning the lapses in safety measures?" He couldn't answer because of shame but he resolved in his mind to comply with the instruction without further delay.

"As a matter of fact, I have spoken about you to my Director and he promised to tell the Permanent Secretary about you."

"*Shege*, Inspector! Me, I will take you to the Emir for introduction. He will tell all chiefs to give you support for you to succeed in your work. You know I can do that."

"Alhaji, I am expecting the President and the Secretary of the Miners' Association of Nigeria by 11:00; it is now 10:55. They will soon be here. *Ehen*, see them coming," Engr. Sluice said, having seen the jeep of the President being driven in. "I hope I am through with you?"

"I like the man!" Alhaji Gogawa said.

"Who did you say you like?"

"The President of the Miners' Association of Nigeria. He wants the Miners' Association to be recognized the more and be empowered. The other day I saw him with the Minister in the Television; he was very composed and confident and I said '*shege, na miji, Oga mu.*'"

"*E don do*, Alhaji. Your own *e no dey* finish. Begin *dey* go, please."

"Inspector, let them come. I will greet them before I go."

ഇറോ

"Good morning, Inspector; you are looking dull. I hope we are welcome," the President of the Miners' Association of Nigeria greeted as he entered.

"You are always welcome. It is just one of those minuses that normally take one to the valley," Engr. Sluice responded.

"You must be on the mountain. You cannot be in the valley while I am here no matter what. Being lively is being healthy," the President encouraged him.

"You are correct," Engr. Sluice agreed and cheered up.

"Alhaji Gogawa, *yaya kake* (how are you)?" the President greeted.

"*Ina lafiya, hukuma hukumai* (I am well, authority of authorities)," responded Alhaji Gogawa.

"*Lafiyarku shine lafiyarmu. Na ji dadi ganin ka kwarai* (Your health is our health. I am really pleased seeing you)," the President said.

"*Haka ni ma shugaba mu na kwarai* (Likewise myself, our reliable leader)," Alhaji Gogawa said and added, "*na san kun zo don Maganar kungiyar mu ne. Ku gaya masa dukan masalolin mu* (I know you come concerning our Association. You should tell him all our problems)."

"*Kar ka damu, Alhaji. Allah ya tamaika* (Don't worry, Alhaji. May God help)," the President said with respect because Alhaji Saminu Gogawa stood firmly for him during his election which was hotly contested.

"Inspector, I am going. Thank you so much for the guidance. *Wallahi* (Of a truth), you are a good man. Don't worry; may God keep us alive. You understand *ba*?"

"Just *dey* go, Alhaji. I am only doing my work as I ought to."

"President, *sai wani lokaci* (till another time)," Alhaji said and left.

ഇൻ

"Now, President, what problem has brought you here?" Engr. Sluice asked the President of the

Miners' Association of Nigeria. He placed the elbow of his left hand on the edge of the table and was scratching the centre of his head with the same hand while jotting something on a piece of paper with his right hand. It could be on the discussion he had with Alhaji Gogawa who had just left his office.

"Many problems, Inspector; I believe you will help us. Members of our Association are finding it difficult to operate in the mines fields."

"I am listening to you; continue," Engr Sluice said, still writing.

"I hope you are listening to me, Inspector. I can see you are still writing."

"If I were not listening, I wouldn't have told you to continue. Do you want me to tell you what you have said? Okay, I won't write again. Continue."

"Thank you. There is the problem of to whom a surface rent should be paid. Is it to the owner of the land, the Traditional Chief or the Government? Our members are confused in this matter, Inspector."

"I am aware of this problem, Mr. President. We are presently handling a case like that in this office. It is from one of the States."

"From which state, Inspector?"

"That is an official matter; you don't need to have the details, Mr. President."

"Then of what use is the Freedom of Information Act, Inspector?"

"Freedom of Information Act does not call for a free fall of stupidity to the detriment of the security of this country. You know there can be some items that are exempted from the Act. This is not the subject matter for this meeting, anyway."

"Okay, but ...," the President still wanted to say something on it but Engr. Sluice was not interested.

"Section 102 of the Act stipulates the payment of surface rent and Section 100 of the Regulations gives effect to it. In both the Act and the Regulations, the beneficiary of the surface rent is referred to as the owner or the occupier of the land which is the subject of the mineral title. To me, an individual, traditional ruler or the government falls in the bracket of owner or occupier of land as the case may be. Look at it this way; if an individual owns or occupies a land either customarily or through purchase, he or she is the owner or occupier of the land and should enjoy the surface rent. If a community has customarily declared some lands such as rocky or hilly areas and the immediate cultivable surrounding land, usually few meters from the foot of the hills as obtainable in some communities, then the traditional rulers are the owners or the occupiers of the land and should logically enjoy the surface rent and, if the area has been designated government reserve, for example, a forest reserve, the government is therefore unquestionably the owner or the occupier of the land and logically it should enjoy the surface rent. That is my understanding and belief on this sensitive matter."

"Are you a lawyer, Inspector?" the Secretary to the Miners' Association asked; he was visibly impressed with the analysis of the owner or occupier of the land.

"Why are you asking?"

"You have really opened my eyes to see the different circumstances the owner or occupier of the land can be determined. This explanation will be helpful in settling disputes concerning payment of the surface rent. You are great, indeed!"

"This is a very simple matter but a volatile one in the mines fields," Engr. Sluice remarked and asked, "President, are you satisfied with the answer?"

"Very well; I will educate our members."

"You have to."

"Inspector, I have another thing to ask you."

"Go on, please."

"Messrs Jungle Mining Limited is mining lead and zinc. The vein of the mineral is underneath and about 30m from the surface. It extends into the area of the Small Scale Mining Lease of No Nonsense Mining Company Limited's Lease. Through lateral spread of the underground mining, Messrs Jungle Mining Limited mined the deposit into No Nonsense Mining Company Limited and a quarrel ensued between the two companies. Is Messrs Jungle Mining Limited not right to have mined the lead/zinc vein since she it is doing it underground?"

"Messrs Mining Jungle Limited was wrong. Section 145 of the Act is very clear on this." He opened to the Section in the Act and read thus; '*Every mineral title, temporary title or mining lease shall be bounded by vertical planes from the surface boundary lines drawn downwards to an unlimited depth from surface.*' Is there any ambiguity here?"

"But No Nonsense Mining Company Limited is mining gold and not lead/zinc, Inspector!" the President said.

"Notwithstanding, it is not within her Lease and the law must be followed, President...."

While Engr. Sluice was with the President of the Miners' Association of Nigeria, the youths of a

107

community somewhere were having a serious problem on payment of surface rent as outlined below.

℘)CB

"We are tired of this cheating! Poor man will not breathe in our community. Everything is determined for the benefit of the Chief. How can the Chief collect the surface rent that belongs to Susami? Is it because he is poor? This time around, we will not allow him to go free with this! Are all of us still of the same mind? Is there any betrayer among us? Let me hear you respond!" Gushi, the leader of the youths spoke, going among them, looking charged for combat. The youths had decided to go and see Engr. Sluice on the issue of their Chief who had denied Susami his right to enjoy surface rent as the owner of the land, the subject of a mineral title.

"All of us are of the same mind. No betrayal! Noretreat! We will not allow the Chief to cheat Susami," the rest of the youths said.

"If someone here is in the camp of the Chief in this matter, let him speak out now or never!" the leader said and beat his chest, saying he was ready to die for justice to reign in the matter.

"Gushi, be assured of my loyalty and commitment to your leadership. However, since you said one can speak out one's mind in this delicate matter, I want to say something," a youth who was a relative of the Chief spoke.

"Ejenpooh, say what you want to say and go straight to the point! We don't have more time to waste! You know in one and half hour's time, we are going to see the Mining Officer."

"Gushi, my leader ...," Ejenpooh began.

"Go straight to the point! Too much of courtesy in addressing me is not my worry," Gushi said and went to sit on a chair, asking for a cigarette to relieve tension in him.

"I just want to say that this matter should be treated with caution."

"A betrayer! Traitor! Is it because you are related to the Chief, the cheat?" Gushi spoke and stood up from the chair and went for Ejenpooh. He slapped him severely. Other youths joined him to beat and kick Ejenpooh. He fainted. He was later revived. When this was going on, a retired Mines Officer in the community arrived on the scene and helped to calm the situation. He told them that since Susami was the owner of the land he inherited from his father, he is the one to enjoy the surface rent.

"We know how courageous you are in telling the truth. You will live long," Gushi said to the retired Mines Officer.

"I respect the Chief but I will not be afraid of telling him the truth because it will be healthy to him and the community," the retired Mines Officer said.

"You will be our Chief one day!" one of the youths said.

"Don't let the Chief hear this. My lineage is not of royal blood. Don't make the Chief look for my head, please."

"He is not serving us but himself and his family!" another youth spoke.

"That is your problem. As for me, I am loyal, and I will continue to be, to the Chief. May I tell you that the President of Miners' Association of Nigeria has gone to see the Inspector of Mines on a matter like this to find out who should collect the surface rent if there is a conflict of this nature. He will be having a meeting with some miners when he is here in three days' time to have a consent letter as stipulated in Section 100 of the Act from the owner(s) of land. He has put in an application for Exploration Licence for precious stones. We have many of them such as garnet, topaz, corundum and emerald in our land. Our land is rich with these treasures. When he comes he will further enlighten you on this matter."

"Because of this, we will no longer go to see the Mining Officer," Gushi announced and said to all, "everybody should return to his house and be ready to answer the Chief when we are called. I know he will look for us," he said and started going away. They dispersed. At that time, Engr. Sluice was still with the President of the Miners' Association of Nigeria.

ॐ

"...Inspector, did I hear you say that a holder of an Exploration Licence can apply for suspension of exploration works?" the President of Miners' Association asked, ready to leave.

"Yes, but under good cause and once annually. Section 42(2) of the Regulations provides for this. More so, under good cause, the Director General of MCO may '*direct that any or part of the period of the suspension shall not be reckoned in the currency of the licence if during that time no work is done by the licence holder....*'That is what Section 42(3) (b) says."

"Many of us don't know this," the Secretary of the Miners' Association of Nigeria said and was particularly happy on the possibility of excluding the period of suspension from the currency of the Licence.

"Yes, because you don't care about reading the law. You can't fight for your rights if you don't know the law," Engr. Sluice said and asked, "is there any question again?"

"Yes, but until another day because I can understand a person is with your Secretary, waiting to see you," the President said. It was Engr. Eugene that had arrived to see him.

"Thanks so much, Inspector; we are leaving now. Next week we will meet in Jos for the Conference of the Nigerian Society of Mining Engineers (NSME)," he said and they left. He still had so many things he wanted to ask for enlightenment on. Engr. Sluice sat, expecting the coming of Engr. Eugene.

ᔕᓍᓂ

"Engr. Eugene, you are here in good time. I like your attribute as to time management," Engr. Sluice commended. "Alice, call Maxwell to come," and he asked Eugene, "how is the quarry? I hope your quarry return for this month will reflect '*the true and correct quantity of mineral won, sold or used, and left on hand.*' Many companies just reflect only the quantity won and sold or reflect used without the left on hand thereby contravening Section 123(b) of the Regulations. You people must always do the right thing for the progress of this country. Adequate statistical figures are essential for good policy making."

"Inspector, but our company has been trying in complying with the provisions of the law. However, I have noted what you said. There will be improvement. Our company will also reflect labour employed in the returns..."

"You are a staff. Go in," Alice said to Maxwell who just came.

111

"Yes, Maxwell, sit down and hear what I am going to tell Engr. Eugene. He is your friend," Engr. Sluice said.

"Okay, sir."

"Under no circumstance, Engr. Eugene, should you again store detonators together with explosives in contravention of Section 22(1) of the Explosives Regulations. As a Mining Engineer, you know why it is so. There can explode if they are kept together. They can only be married together by a short firer, the Blaster, during blasting operation and not during storage. I will deal heavily with your company if you do not build a detonator store as I have instructed."

"If we get money we will comply with your instruction, sir," Eugene said.

"Don't tell me that! I can't understand why companies will spend millions of naira in public relations but can't do the right thing at the site! They prefer to bribe people instead of doing the right thing. This must be stopped!"

"But, sir, the Management is seriously complaining of lack of funds now."

"I say don't tell me this! Every blessed day, dump trucks line up for aggregates at your quarry. What is your company doing with the money? Did I not hear a construction company has recently made a down payment of fifty million naira to your company for stone aggregates? How much will it take to build a Detonator Store? You must do something about it. I give you the grace of one month and two days. Maxwell, you must write a third reminder to the company tomorrow on this matter."

"Okay, sir."

"Engr. Eugene, this matter is closed except if you have any other thing to say."

"Inspector, you should do something to ease our problem of buying and transferring explosives."

"The Ministry is doing something about it, taking into consideration the present security challenges in the country," he said and turning to Maxwell, he instructed, "write the reminder and let him take it with him as he goes back. He must wait to collect it. Don't go and write too much English. Just refer them to our first letter and the reminders. Ask the company to comply with our instruction within one month and two days of the receipt of the letter, stating the consequences of continuous lack of compliance. Go with him, Eugene."

EIGHT

Engr. Russo Sluice, the energetic Inspector of Mines, always loves reading the history of mining in Nigeria. One day, while sitting in his office, he was reading a historical bulletin on tin mining on the Plateaus. He came across the information on the camp beds and the bush lamps used by the British, the Indian and the Nigerian Mining Engineers understudying them during field inspections in the years when mining was booming. Mention was also made of the Mines Police who effectively maintained peace in the mines fields. They ensured that offences such as salting, use of false or fraudulent scales and illegal mining were hardly committed. He sighed as he remembered that draglines with big buckets were no longer dominating the mining paddocks to scoop cassiterite (tin ore) for processing. He also remembered the days when Makeri smelting company was operating at high capacity. He was worried because the mining industry is now crawling instead of walking on its feet. In the past, it was walking side by side with agriculture. Both were the mainstay of the Nigerian Economy.

It was in the above mood, he opened to Section 134 of the Act to read about the offence of salting. Salting is the act of deceiving any person on the richness of a mineral deposit by fraudulently placing or caused to be placed minerals in the area; or mingling or caused to be mingled fake substances with mineral ores or samples to enhance their nature and any other similar action. This offence was so repugnant to Engr. Sluice that he shouted; *"Just for money! Just for money! That is wickedness.*" He wished that the fine of ₦500,000.00 or the imprisonment for a term not exceeding two years for a convicted person on the offence of salting as stipulated in Section 134(b) of the Act would be reviewed upwards and such convicted persons be banned forever from the mines fields as they could be rightly termed pollutants of the mining environment against investors or its survival.

"Sir, what is the problem?" Alice rushed in and asked Engr. Sluice. She had heard him shouting.

"Oh, Alice, there is nothing that has really happened. I am only upset by the fraudulent activities of some miners in the mines fields. They are detrimental to the industry. Call Johnson and Maxwell to come. Is my cup of tea ready?"

"As a matter of fact, I have just plugged the kettle into the socket. It will soon be ready, sir. And …,"

"What do you want to say again, Alice?"

"You will have to buy a tin of the powdered peak milk tomorrow. What remains is only for today and tomorrow. The coffee can last for another week."

"No problem. You can just have the money for that now. Make sure it is not an expired one," he said and gave her the money. Alice would always like to be sent by Engr. Sluice to buy things for him as he hardly collected the change from her. She had once bought an expensive dress from such small changes which she had disciplined herself to save over a long period of time.

"Alice, remember to call Johnson and Maxwell for me," he reminded her as she was walking out of his office.

"I have not forgotten, sir."

"Okay."

On the instruction of Engr. Sluice, the previous day, Johnson and Maxwell were drafting a letter to a company which had contravened Section 18(2) of the Regulations by not keeping '*correct plans of exploration...,*' and refusing to '*provide to the Nigerian Geological Survey Agency for storage and archiving, a complete set of all geo-scientific data... maps, coring and samples*' as stipulated in Section 43(d) of the Act. Engr. Sluice would not tolerate any laxity that would not allow a reliable data base of minerals to be built for the country as it is a tool to woo investors. While they were doing this, Alice came in and told them:

"Johnson, Maxwell, *Oga* is calling the two of you. You must run to see him."

"Run? *Say wetin* happen? You, this girl, will not stop talking to your seniors in arrogance. Mr. Idowu, thank God you are here. You will have to give a query to this stubborn girl on her lack of manners when speaking to her seniors," Maxwell said while Johnson was smiling. Mr. Idowu was a Higher Executive Officer with an athletic stature.

"As a matter of fact, I have been thinking of giving her a query for always closing before time whenever Engr. Sluice travels."

"You, too, Idowu? You want my trouble? Don't follow Maxwell to be a bad man. Maxwell is always confused," she said and left, majestically cat-walking like a girl in a beauty contest so as to provoke Maxwell to anger.

"Maxwell, let us go and see *Oga*," Johnson said and asked Idowu to pick from the ground, a detached leaf of the Act which contains Section 98 that prohibits exploration or mining of minerals in sacred areas and injuring or destroying any object of veneration. The constructors of the mining laws had sensitively done well in this provision as tampering with areas and objects of worship in the Nigerian religious terrain could easily spark riots.

"Yes, you people have finally come. Anytime I send for you, you must immediately stop what you are doing and come. You get me?" Engr. Sluice said and continued to read a letter on a company's employment mix of 40 Nigerians to 20 Foreigners which was not good.

"Okay, sir."

He finished reading the letter and said, "It has just occurred to me this morning that I have to send you to inspect the mine of Mr. Mike Emu. He has continuously violated the provisions of the Act and the Regulations. The company shall be sanctioned in accordance with the provisions of Section 20(3) of the Regulations. Maxwell, take the Regulations and read that portion," he said and handed a copy of the Regulations to him.

'*Where a mineral title holder continues to violate provisions of the Act and these Regulations with respect to environmental protection, mine operations, safety regulations, or the provisions of its environmental protection plan, the exploration and mining activities of such a holder shall be suspended for up to sixty days, and if such deficiencies are not eliminated within this period, the exploration activities of the mineral title holder shall be terminated or, in case of an operating mine, shall be closed,*' Maxwell read.

"That is well read, Maxwell. Based on your fluency and command of the English language and your ability for talking a lot, you are supposed to be in the court room, arguing cases for people. That is by the way, anyway. It is now almost sixty days since we suspended mining operations in Mr. Emu's mine due to some deficiencies of which you know. Go and inspect it to see the level of elimination of the deficiencies especially on tailing disposal. You have to go right now. Jegede will take you there. Mr. Emu's mine plan does not reflect *potential cases of health hazards to be encountered in* his *mining... activities and the proposed mitigation plans* as stipulated in Section 141 of the Regulations. I will write to him on that. Start going now."

"Sir, how do we treat this case of Messrs Intelligent Mining Investment Ltd?" Johnson asked. Messrs Intelligent Mining Investment Ltd had been mining Kaolin without the requisite mining papers.

"Why did you ask *Oga* that simple question? We shall make the company pay royalty. It is that simple," Maxwell said, feeling good that he had said the right thing.

"You boys can shame the Ministry in a court of law and anywhere; *chai*," Engr. Sluice was annoyed.

"Sir, how can we shame the Ministry?" Maxwell asked. He was not calm like Johnson. He had a pathetic and variable social life that he has not been able to tame.

"Shut up your mouth! How can you collect royalty from an illegal miner? Do you want to encourage illegal mining? Oh, no; oh, no; the work has spoiled," Engr. Sluice bewailed.

As they were talking, the Mines Manager of the company, Sadiq Faisal, came in.

"Sadiq *na* your *papa* born you. We just *dey* talk about your company and you came in. What a coincidence? You are welcome!" Engr. Sluice said.

"Thanks. I am here to pay the royalty on the Kaolin we have mined," Sadiq Faisal said, thinking Engr. Sluice would be happy with that.

"Sadiq, your case is that of illegal mining without the requisite papers. Your case is being treated under Section 20(1)(i) of the Regulations. We are not collecting royalty from your company but all income or products you have gotten from this illegal mining shall be confiscated and a fine doubling the value of the minerals you have mined will be imposed on you. In this case, you will have to truthfully avail to this office the quantity of the mineral you have mined for us to assess its value."

"Sir, but, but," he turned and glanced at Maxwell, "Maxwell has told us that it is royalty we are to pay. Why has this changed now? My Management is already happy that we are getting over this embarrassing matter!"

"Sadiq, that is what the law says; nothing can be done about that," he said and turned and looked at Maxwell with suppressed anger.

"I will relate this new development to the Management."

"You had better do that, please."

"You will hear from us the soonest, Inspector."

"There should be no more delay on this matter; Okay?"

"Yes, Inspector," Sadiq Faisal answered and left.

ഇറ

"Maxwell, I am wrong to have said that you should have been a Lawyer. You would have been a very bad and volatile one. Did I send you to speak on this sensitive matter with the company? Do you have vested interest in the matter? If you had wanted to impress the company, you should have checked what the law says on that! Johnson, you should advise him to be careful. This is a disgrace to this office," Engr. Sluice said and asked them to leave immediately for the inspection. They complied and Engr. Sluice sat quietly for quite some time, thinking about the future management of the mines fields as an old man who is about to die thinks of how his family would be like after his death. He remembered how Engr. Inuwa Gombe, P. C. Okonkwo, Henry k. Erewa, J. D. A. Omalu and Damian A. Korie, and those that came after them such as J .B. D. Pam, I. D. Yahaya, M. K. Amate, Olumuyiwa Ige, D. F. Attandu, G. J. A. Agbo, J. S. N. Mgbachi, B. C. Ofodum, S. O. Oladipo, I. A. Lawal and T. F. Oluwafemi and others made references to the mining laws with ease like a Professor Emeritus. He imagined himself in that era of grandeur of the mining industry when the mining giants such as Almagamated Tin Mines and Consolidated Tin Mines dominated the tin mines of the Plateaus and wished things could be like that again. He also recalled the years Mines Officers usually attended the annual conference of the Association of Tin Producing Countries (ATPC). It was in this mood he remembered he had an appointment with the Director-General of the Mining Cadastre Office that morning. He sighed as he took his mind off from such fantastic and historical images and decided to call the Director-General as they had arranged.

"Good morning, sir," Engr. Sluice greeted.

"Engr. Sluice, how are you?" the Director-General responded from the other end.

Engr. Sluice heard the Director-General in the background telling someone that a company's Mining Lease would be revoked because he had been notified by the Mines Inspectorate Department, in exercising the power bestowed on it by Section 66(2) of the Regulations, that the company had contravened Section 66(1) of the Regulations by not meeting the prescribed reporting requirements on a Mining Lease in line with schedule 5.

"Sir, are you with me?" Engr. Sluice asked as he could hear in the background the man pleading with the Director-General for leniency.

"Yes, Engineer, go on please," and said to the man from the company before him, "just give me three minutes, please."

"Sir, it is not the fault of the Mines Inspectorate Department in the delay of the processing of the renewal of mineral title applications as wrongly alleged in some quarters. Companies have not been complying adequately with the provisions of Regulation 18 concerning information and reporting. For example, Index New Generation Mines Limited is going round accusing the Department wrongly on the delay of the renewal of its Exploration Licence at Uner while all efforts made for her to forward to us the half yearly reports of expenditure on its exploration works in compliance with Regulation 18(1)(e) has not been successful. That is one of our problems in the processing of applications for the renewal of mineral titles. The Director of Mines

Inspectorate Department is disturbed on this. Our Department is committed to providing an enabling environment for all players in the mining industry and in its contribution to the growth of the GDP of this nation."

"Engr. Sluice, I am aware of this problem. However, do your very best to send the progress reports so that the Minister will not speak on this again," the Director-General said and turned to the man from the company and said to him, "Mr. Man, that is the position of your mineral title. I am going for a meeting with the Minister and investors from the Islamic Republic of Iran." The investors were interested in copper. Their company, Global Mining Giant Plc, was globally known to protect vegetation and the landscape of a mining site as demanded by Section 157 of the Regulations. It was also known to be keen in the protection of top soil so as not to trigger erosion; conservation of biodiversity, National parks, cultural heritage and sanctuaries; protection of flora and fauna; protection of endangered species ... and, the prevention of pollution of the environment as required by Regulations 158, 159, 160, 161 and 162 respectively. This was one of the reasons the Minister was interested in them investing in the Minerals industry in the country.

As the Director-General from the other end was going for the meeting with the Minister, Engr. Sluice received a team of Civil Engineers led by Engr. Structural Phenomenon, Director of Civil Engineering, from the Ministry of Power, Works and Housing. He had known the Director during a meeting they held sometime ago when a staff of the Ministry of Power, Works and Housing had told a Mines officer on a mission to make a company pay royalty on laterite that laterite was not a mineral and as such royalty should not be demanded from the company. An argument ensued between them in front of the Project Manager of the company, a foreigner, to his dismay, as to why two officials representing the same government with a single purpose of national development as different channels of river empty into the same ocean, could not understand one another. However, he wished he would not pay the royalty as payment of taxes is not joyfully done anywhere in the world but its evasion is loved so as to maximize profits. Engr. Sluice and Engr. Phenomenon had met to discuss the matter. During that meeting, Engr. Sluice had referred Engr. Phenomenon to Section 75 of the Act in which laterite is listed among the quarriable minerals and by this, he was silenced.

ೠೠ

"Engr. Phenomenon, you are welcome," Engr. Sluice said.

"Thank, you," Engr. Phenomenon responded, not looking happy. Engr. Sluice wondered what could be wrong.

"Hope, there is no problem, Engineer? You are looking so serious and not happy. What is the problem?"

"Do you have to ask me when you have sent your boys to disturb Messrs Highway Construction Ltd? Must your office and ours always have conflicts? Mr. President has personally instructed the company to complete and handover this project as scheduled. It is time lined. Why must you do this, Sluice?" he fumed.

"What is really the matter, Engr. Phenomenon? Let us speak as matured and senior officers. We must groom these young ones to be calm in handling situations by example. That will make them to reason. So, calm down and let me know the problem." Those that came with Engr. Phenomenon admired the calmness of Engr. Sluice which was to the shame of Engr. Phenomenon who was always harsh with them.

"Why should your staff demand from the company the payment of royalty on a highway cut which was not meant for commercial purpose and therefore not mining? Why are you also planning to stop the company from working?"

"Alice, has Johnson come back?" Engr. Sluice called and asked. He had sent Johnson to deliver a letter to a company which had contravened Section 191 of the Regulations by not preparing a mine waste disposal plan, establish waste water retention and treatment techniques and ensure safe management of contaminated runoff and ground water contamination. In the letter, the company was asked to deal with the deficiencies or risk closure. He had also sent Maxwell with a letter of a query to another company for closing and abandoning their mine without applying not less than three (3) months to the date of closure and abandonment to the Mines Environmental Compliance Department and sending the copies to Mines Inspectorate Department and Mining Cadastre Office thereby contravening Section 217 of the Regulations.

"Yes, I saw him passing just now," Alice answered.

"Call him to come quickly, please. Just hold on. Let my boy come," he said to Engr. Phenomenon. They kept quiet as they waited for Johnson.

"*Ehen*, Johnson, what did you tell me about Messrs Highway Construction Ltd concerning excavating laterite along the Mile 2 – Kurmin Jibrin road project?" Engr. Sluice asked.

"Sir, on the day I went there, the company excavated the laterite and sold to people with commercial dump trucks. They collected money from them. It wasn't just a high-cut or cut-and-dump sort of thing."

"It is not so!" Engr. Phenomenon fumed.

'Calm down, Engr. Phenomenon. Many funny things happen in the field without the knowledge of Management. The Project Manager and you might not have known this. Your boys who are supervising the construction of the road might have connived with the workers to do this. Don't you think so, Engineer?" Engr. Sluice said this not knowing he had hit the nail on the head as one of the people that came with Engr. Phenomenon had connived in the sale of the laterite. He nearly betrayed himself by his body language as he became restless, hoping Johnson would not mention his name as an accomplice. Johnson nearly did so.

"Sir...," Johnson tried to mention the jittery man's name as one of the people who were collecting money that day.

"It is alright, Johnson, you can go," Engr. Sluice cut him off without knowing Johnson was about to give an important information that would have shamed Engr. Phenomenon to the bones.

"Okay, sir," he said and briefly looked at the jittery man. Their eyes locked and Johnson could see the fear in his face.

"As a matter of fact, it is a highway cut and not commercial quarrying," Engr. Phenomenon said, looking sober now.

"We will look into the matter and treat it vis-à-vis the provisions and dictates of Section 170 of the

Regulations which exempts materials excavated primarily for a non-mining purpose from being termed as mining operation, and from subjection to the fulfillment of the requirement of the Regulations so long they are not sold commercially."

"That will be good," Engr. Phenomenon said.

"But Engineer, come; why didn't the Project Manager come by himself on this matter? You are not supposed to be here on this matter. I hope you understand me?" Engr. Sluice said.

"I do, but remember, as a Director of Civil Engineering, I am concerned about job delivery as scheduled. In this case, I am right to intervene. You must understand this."

"It is okay. However, I will not listen to you again on this matter except Mr. Crusher, the Project Manager, comes by himself. He is the one to pay the royalty and not your Ministry should we finally confirm the company is into commercial quarrying of the laterite."

"No problem," Engr. Phenomenon responded and begged to leave, thinking that he had made a point no matter what.

"That is alright; go well," Engr. Sluice said and leisurely started to sketch on a paper, a square of a cadastral unit of dimensions 15″ x 15″ as given in Section 106 of the Regulations. An engineering pencil was always by his side.... At almost the same time, Johnson and Maxwell were already at Mr. Emu's mining site, arguing with the security guards.

ഇൽ

"You cannot prevent us from entering this mine! Do you know we are Mines Officers who are empowered by Sections 6, 121 and 122 of the

Regulations to inspect the mines? You are contravening these Regulations. We must inspect this mine today!" Maxwell spoke in anger to the security guards who said the Mines Manager was not around as he had accompanied Mr. Mike Emu to see a Customs Officer in charge of a port (sea).The Customs Officer had seized 305 ounces of gold belonging to Mr. Emu which was being exported to the state of Alaska in the USA without an Export Permit. The Customs Officer had been empowered by Section 132(3) of the Regulations to do that. However, the Customs Officer had himself contravened Section 132(4) of the Regulations by not conveying the seized quantity of the gold to the Mines Inspectorate Department within 72 hours of the seizure. It was now five days the seized gold had been with him.

"If you don't allow us to inspect the mine today, you will be sanctioned in line with Section 20(6) of the Regulations. Open the gate!" Maxwell continued to fume. Section 20(6) of the Regulations says:

'A Federal High Court may impose a fine of up to a sum ranging between one hundred and fifty thousand naira on any person or group of persons who intentionally prevent or obstruct an authorized inspector of mines or official(s) of the Ministry from performing their duties in the course of an inspection of an exploration or mining operation.'

"Maxwell, let me handle this," Johnson said and told the security guards to call Mr. Emu and tell him of their presence and mission to the mine.

"*Oga, na* some two people *dey* give us problem here. They say they *be* mining people from town and want to enter mining area. We say no and they want to fight us," a security guard spoke to Mr. Emu using Airtel network, the only available network at the site.

"Who are they? Let me speak to them?" Mr. Emu shouted from the other end.

"Take, *Oga wan* talk to you?" Johnson collected the mobile phone.

"Good morning, sir," Johnson greeted.

"Who are you and from where?" Mr. Emu asked.

"I am Johnson from the Ministry of Mines and Steel Development. I am here with Maxwell. Engr. Sluice has sent us to come and inspect your mine."

"Johnson! How is Engr. Sluice?

"He is doing fine, sir."

"I am happy to hear that. But you did not notify us of your coming and as such you cannot inspect the mine. I hope you know that?"

"We must not always inform you before we come for inspection, sir."

"Why? You mean you can visit one's property anyhow?"

"Sir, Section 121 of the Regulations, among other things, empowers Mines Officers, with or without any notice, to visit a mining area or a mine to inspect it. It is your obligation to allow us to do that as provided for in Section 22(xi) of the Regulations."

"You people with your laws. Let me speak with the security man."

"Okay, sir."

"Allow them to enter and do what they want. Davis is there to attend to them."

"You can go in. Davis, the firing man *dey* there for you."

"*Wetin* Davis *dey* fire?" Johnson asked.

"Im dey fire bomb to pieces the rock *wey dey* carry gold. Even yesterday, *im* fired two times; in the morning and afternoon," the security guard spoke not knowing the company had been carrying out the blasting operations at the site against the instruction of Engr. Sluice. Mr. Emu had been instructed to suspend blasting operations in the mine until he complied with the standard provisions of Section 35(1)(a) of the Explosives Regulations by building an adequate sand or earth bank as the initial one had been heavily eroded. They went and saw Davis.

ഇരു

Davis took them round the mine and they saw that the previously observed deficiencies had not been eliminated. This was not a thing of surprise to Johnson and Maxwell as Mr. Emu was known to be notoriously stubborn in not complying with instructions.

"Davis, when did you carry out blasting operation last in this mine?" Maxwell asked.

"Since you stopped us we have not done any blasting. It is about six months now," he lied not knowing the security guard had revealed their secret. They crush and process the ore in the night.

The inspection showed that the company had completely ignored the instruction of the Ministry to eliminate the deficiencies which include lack of proper drainage for accumulated water from an active dump as prescribed in Section 196 of the Regulations.

From all indications, the recommendation of Johnson and Maxwell to Engr. Sluice on the inspection report they would give would be that of a revocation which would be notified to the Mining Cadastre Office through appropriate channels....

"Alice, Johnson and Maxwell are supposed to have returned by now. I hope they will soon be here," Engr. Sluice said.

"They have just returned. I saw Johnson coming in."

"Oh, that is good; you know when one sends his staff on field work, one does not rest until one sees them returned safely."

"He should be the one knocking the door, sir."

Johnson entered.

"Johnson, you are back? That is good. How was the trip?"

"Very hectic as usual; field work is always so."

"Tell me what happened."

"*Oga*, Mr. Emu will never change! He is still the Mr. Emu we know. Can he ever change? I find it difficult to believe that he will change."

"Tell me exactly what happened, Johnson."

"He has not eliminated any of the deficiencies! Do you know he still carries out blasting operations? Yesterday they blasted twice! The security guard told us. On tactical enquiry, Davis, the shot firer, lied to us that the company stopped blasting operations since we suspended their mining operations. Anyway, the inspection report will be given to you tomorrow."

"You must write it quickly and recommend for the revocation of the Mining Lease. As for Davis, the blasting certificate in his name shall be revoked in accordance with the provisions of Section 44(4) of the Explosives Regulations of 1967. There is no going back on this. They think one is stupid by being gracious to them all this while. We just want to move the minerals industry forward to contribute substantially to the GDP of this country. That is all!" Engr. Sluice fumed. He will fulfill what he had spoken since Mr. Mike Emu had ignored his instructions which were based on the provision of Section 120 of the Regulations which empowers the Director of Mines Inspectorate to issue certain orders so as to stop violation of the provisions of the Act and the Regulations. Mr. Emu had added salt to his wound by not remedying the deficiencies and refraining from carrying out the mining activities. He would also have to tell Engr. Sluice the source of the explosives he used in the blasting operations since, at the time, the instruction was given to him to stop working and to remedy the deficiencies; he had completely exhausted the stock of explosives and all accessories. That was a steep and slippery mountain before him. How he would surmount it is left to the imagination.

NINE

"Johnson, this is the exact location where those people were lifting the laterite. I mean the people we saw when we were coming from Kun," Engr. Sluice said while looking at a topographical map of a scale of 1:100,000. A preferable quadrant of the map, in a scale of 1:50,000, which covered the area was not available.

"Yes, I understand, sir. You know there is a stream that passes close to where they are mining the laterite. See it here. It is exactly as seen in the field, flowing in the North-West direction."

"Good; you and Maxwell will go there with a team of the Nigerian Security and Civil Defence Corps (NSCDC) to stop them working. I hope you do know that one of the duties of the NSCDC is to protect the natural resources of this nation. That is why our Ministry is working in synergy with it to sanitize the mining industry. Where is Maxwell?"

"Can I go and call him for you?"

"Yes; it is very necessary for him to be here," he said and wondered why mineral operators were careless about observing environmental mining laws. He had been assigned an adhoc duty by the Minister of State of the Ministry to carry out inspection of mining sites within his jurisdiction and report as soon as possible on the level of environmental compliance. The Mines Environmental Officer for the zone had gone on leave.

"Here is Maxwell," Johnson said.

"Maxwell, come closer. You see this point?"

"Yes, sir."

"This is where those people we saw the other day as we were returning from Kun are lifting the laterite. I have told Johnson that both of you and well-armed personnel of the Nigerian Security and Civil Defence Corps (NSCDC) will be there today to make some arrests. There is no lease over that area. I am very sure of this."

"Okay, sir."

"Maxwell, go and stand by the door and see who is speaking with the security guards. I can hear their voices raised high."

"Okay, sir."

"Johnson, you know Section 115(2) of the Regulations says a mineral title holder should prepare a plan of mining operations and submit to the Mines Inspectorate Department, Mining Cadastre Office and Mines Environmental Compliance Department before commencement of operations."

"Okay ..."

"Yes, that is what the law says. Many companies have not been complying with this."

"We must enforce this, sir."

"Of course, Johnson; we hope adequate logistics will be provided to enable us function as we should. That is our problem and you are aware of it."

"This is a constant problem in our monthly reports to the Director of Mines which is transmitted to Management," Johnson said. He was the one that always compiled the monthly report of activities.

"Almost all the companies often start work without the placement of demarcation point markers in compliance with the provisions of Section 118(1)(b) of the Regulations. In fact, many of them do not comply with most of the Regulations such as obtaining a copy of approved Environmental Impact

Assessment (EIA), building a detailed work programme and submitting a copy of Community Development Agreement (CDA)."

"*Oga*, we must sanction them on this," Johnson said, sounding like a militant Mines Officer.

"It is not that we don't want to do that, Johnson. These are some of the teething problems of the gradual restoration of the mining industry to its past glory. We must apply the law with caution so as not to discourage struggling investors."

"Sir, there is need to bend the stick to your desire when it is still fresh. You can't do that when it is dried; you know what I mean."

"Don't worry; gradually we will make them comply with the mining laws," Engr. Sluice said. He told Johnson that the Ministry was considering inviting Ease of Mining Limited for equipment leasing collaboration. The company had its corporate Headquarters in Port Harcourt and had been widely explored by the mining sector. In her active inventory were earth-moving equipment such as Bulldozers, Wheel Loaders and Excavators, Caterpillar Excavator model 320 BL, Caterpillar D5 Bulldozer and Caterpillar Bulldozer model D7H with ripper. Engr. Sluice had read that in a newspaper the previous day....

The security guards were still talking in high voices with a man at the gate.

ৡটিজ্ঞ

"You must stop for us to check your motor for security risk items," the Chief Security Officer of the office said and ordered one of the security guards not to open the gate.

"Pam, don't you recognize me again? How can I, Maru, carry bad things and come to this office?"

"*Oga* has told us to check everybody; big man or small man; even the staff of this office. You *no* hear bomb exploded yesterday in Allow Everybody In Ltd? Many people died there."

"Open the gate for us to go in; we are friends," Maru insisted.

"*Oga*, you want me to lose my job because we are friends? I *no go gree* with this *lai-lai*."

"Stubborn person, check and see whether I carry any dangerous thing in this car," Maru finally succumbed.

"*Na* you *sabi* that one; I must do my work," Pam said and applied the metal detector on Maru's car and then allowed him in....

ಬಂಡ

"*Oga*, it is Alhaji Maru and some people that are quarrelling with the security guards. They are coming, sir," Maxwell reported and said many animals and vegetation were dying in one tantalite mining site because the company had contravened Section 124 of the Act by not making provisions to ensure that the water used in the milling and concentration of the tantalite did not contain injurious substances of levels detrimental to the animals and the vegetation before being discharged from the mine.

"Maxwell, I am happy that you can now speak and make reference to the mining laws. Keep on improving in that regard," Engr. Sluice commended and turned to welcome Alhaji Maru who had just come in.

"Alhaji Maru, you are here today. It has been a long time. Did you travel out of the country? I have

135

been looking for you to find out why you have stopped the mining operation. Sit down. You are very much welcome," Engr. Sluice said.

"Inspector, I am very surprised that you told your security guards to check me! Do you see me as a person who is dangerous? Am I a bad man? I may stop coming to this office in person," Alhaji. Maru complained.

"Alhaji Maru, why are you talking as if you don't know what the country is passing through now in terms of security challenges everywhere. No one is sure of anybody. This thing we are doing is even for your own good. Assuming as we are sitting now and my security guards become careless and allow a known but unsuspected dangerous man in, all of us will be affected. You should understand this and co-operate with us anytime you come, please."

"*Haba*, I feel very bad about this. I am known here very well," Alhaji Maru kept on complaining.

"So, let me hear you Alhaji. It is now over six months that you stopped working at the mine. Why?"

"I stopped the mining operations in my mine because the international market demand for tantalite is very low now. If I should continue, it will be at a loss. To maintain Chinese staff is very costly. You know I have been given an expatriate qouta of 10 Chinese nationals and having over 40 Nigerians working in the mine. Presently, I owe them two month's salary arrears. I can't continue with this. They have families to take care of. That was why I closed the mine."

"You should have informed this office of this before now in compliance with the provisions of Section 65 of the Regulations."

"What does it say, Inspector?" Engr. Mustapha who had come with Alhaji Maru asked. He was the Mines Manager of the company.

"Don't ask me that question, Engineer! What is the use of having the copy of the Act and the Regulations with you? Is it just for you to decorate your table?"

"Inspector, forget about him and tell us. He is not serious. He is already on his way out of the company. When I resume operations in the mine, you can recommend another Mining Engineer to me."

Section 65(1) of the Regulations says if a company stops mining operations for 6 months, it should inform the Mines Inspectorate Department and give the reasons for stopping work and the Department may give him technical advice. If the stoppage gets to 36 months, the Department can investigate and recommend appropriate measures to be taken to the Mining Cadastre Office."

"For the Mining Casdastre Office to do what?"

"The Mines Inspectorate Department may recommend revocation of the mineral title if no good cause is shown for the stoppage."

"Well, I will bring a letter on this tomorrow in compliance with the law."

"Engr. Sluice, I will submit my letter of resignation to the company tomorrow. One company that knows my worth has been courting me to join it. I was dragging my feet to join it but since Alhaji does not appreciate my sacrifice to his company, let him consider me to have resigned. These people don't understand that Mining Engineers are making money for them. What is there? I can start my own small mine and grow. Is it not about taking risk? I am not

137

happy with you, Alhaji. After all the things I have done for the company? No, no; I can't tolerate this," Engr. Mustapha said, leaving the office.

"Where are you going, Engineer Mustapha? Come back!" Engr. Sluice said.

"No, Inspector! I can't bear this in your presence. It is a disgrace to me! Does he think I will die if he sacks me?"

"Let him go, Inspector," Alhaji Maru said and inwardly worried to have embarrassed Engr. Mustapha before Engr. Sluice. As a Sanguine, he often spoke spontaneously and always regretted it later.

"Alhaji Maru, as a matter of fact, Mustapha is one of the best Mining Engineers we have around. Remember he is a well trained Mining Engineer."

"*Haba?*"

"Yes, Alhaji; the company that wants to snatch him away from you has heard about him."

"I will settle with him. After having sent him to South Africa and Australia for training, I can't just lose him like that," Alhaji Maru said. However, Mustapha was done with him. He had an independent mind and was always firm when he takes a decision. It was not he that would regret but Alhaji Maru, the investor.

"Please, do that as soon as possible."

"Inspector, until I bring the letter tomorrow," he said and stood up to go out of the office.

"I will be expecting you."

"Alright," he said and left to meet his driver, Nasiru, and Mustapha, waiting for him outside.

ഇൽ

"Nasiru, where is Engr. Mustapha?" Alhaji Maru asked his driver.

"He is already inside the car."

"Enter and let us go back." Nasiru started the engine and off they left. The return journey was not to be as lively as when they were coming. Alhaji Maru had embittered Mustapha and put himself in confusion and shame as he would have to lower his voice before Mustapha to convince him not to resign from his company.

𝒮𝒞𝒳

It was when Alhaji Maru had left that Engr. Sluice realised he had forgotten to remind him to reclaim and restore the mined out area as stipulated in Section 156 of the Regulations and to tell his friend, Mr. Tobi, who had violated the provisions of Section 152(3)(iv)(a,c,e,k and n) of the Regulations by not featuring the subjects of climate condition, hydrology, soil chemistry, air quality and project potential environmental impacts in the Environmental Impact Assessment statement he submitted in hard copy to the Ministry, to come the following day to see him.

"Johnson, you and Maxwell should start going now; Kun is far. I have just spoken to the State Co-ordinator of the Nigerian Security and Civil Defence Corps (NSCDC), Mr. Ebere; his boys are already waiting for you. Meet them in their office. Call Jedege, please. Yes, Maxwell, stay back. Let Johnson call him; you and Jegede *no dey gree at all*. Small mistake, the two of you will start quarrelling now and for nothing. I don't know the problem between the two of you."

Johnson dashed to call Jegede. He came.

"Do you have enough fuel in the car to take you to Kun and back?" Engr. Sluice asked Jegede.

"I think so, sir."

"You have started again. Answer me correctly. Do you have enough fuel to take you to Kun and equally bring you back?"

"Yes, sir."

"Now you have said something. Johnson, take three thousand naira (₦3,000.00) in case you will need more fuel."

"Thank you, sir."

"Start going, and good luck," he said and decided to complete a letter on Mine Waste Management he was writing to a company to prepare their mine waste disposal plan and establish waste water retention and treatment techniques in compliance with the provisions of Section 191 of the Regulations....

℘℘℘

At about 20 kilometers to Kun, there was a Kaolin quarry owned by a company called Aiding the Pharmaceuticals Ltd which was about 300 metres off the road to the West. When they got there, Johnson asked Jegede to stop the car. At the instance of Engr. Sluice, he wanted to see the Quarry Manager, Engr. Luke Pit, a Nigerian citizen by birth, to ask him to forward to the Minister the certificate of the result of Kaolin specimen the company had been given permit in accordance with the provisions of Section 132 of the Regulations to export to Canada for scientific analysis. The permit was granted to the company eight months ago and the company ought to have forwarded the certificate within six (6) months of the export of the specimen in compliance with the provisions of

Section 144 of the Act. Could the company have dubiously turned the specimen into a commercial item while in Canada? That was the thought that was occupying the mind of Engr. Sluice.

As they stopped the vehicle, they could see people fighting at the quarry and bags filled with Kaolin were all over the place. Shouts were heard. The Nigerian Security and Civil Defence Corps that went with them rushed to maintain peace.

"All of you should stop fighting! Anybody that refuses to listen will face the consequences," the most senior officer of the Corps warned.

"Officer, this company has spoiled our environment! Many of our animals have died in these holes they dug! Some children have fallen into some of the holes! We don't want them anymore here! They must leave our land," the President of the community, Adamu, said.

"It is unfortunate that these things are happening but you people shouldn't have taken the law into your hands. We thank God that no weapon was used as you were fighting. It would have been a different story by now. You may wish to note that obstructing a holder of a mineral title to operate is an offence which attracts a fine of not more than ₦500,000.00 or imprisonment of not more than 2 years or both when it is first committed," Johnson said and tried to remember the mining law on this. He could not. It is Section 138(2)(a) of the Act.

"Adamu, didn't I tell you people that my company is planning to rehabilitate the mined out area? Why couldn't your community be patient? Some communities are praying for investment of this nature in their area but can't have it. Your community is

141

lucky but you are sending us away," Engr. Pit said, shaking his head.

As they were talking, a 30-ton trailer came to the quarry to load Kaolin to Calabar.

"No loading of Kaolin today! We will not agree until you reclaim these holes," Adamu said and asked some boys to stop the trailer from being loaded.

"You have to allow the trailer to be loaded. It has been paid to come. Do you want the company in Calabar to lose?" Johnson spoke.

They finally agreed and the trailer was loaded with the Kaolin. Johnson told Engr. Pit of the need to forward the certificate of the analysis of the specimen to the Ministry and they continued with the journey to Kun. While they were going, Johnson told Maxwell what was going on in the Ministry.

∞∞

"Maxwell, *Oga*, Engr. Sluice, told me the Minister has approved that the Director-General, Mining Cadastre Office, the Director of Mines and he should attend the Prospectors and Developers Association of Miners, Canada (PDAC) forum in Toronto, coming up next month," Johnson said.

"What is the forum about?" Maxwell asked. He had been careless and did not know about this very important forum.

"Engr. Sluice said that it is the World's Largest Mining Forum usually organized by the Prospectors and Developers Association of Canada. He said miners, industries and governments usually attend this forum to discuss about how to improve on the activities of the mining sector. Here, people network to get businesses during entrepreneur cocktail dinner."

"Yes, *Oga* told me that he and the Director-General of the Mining Cadastre Office are going to Canada very soon; yes, *na* two days ago he told me this. He was very happy. *Im* say e *go* get big pocket money," Jegede said, not concentrating so much on driving the car. He nearly brushed an open pick-up car loaded with goats going the opposite direction. It was going to a certain market to sell them.

"Jegede, you too *dey* put mouth nearly in everything we *dey* talk. See how you nearly collide with this pick-up car. Your own is to drive with caution," Maxwell complained.

"Maxwell, you *don* come with your *wahala* again. *Me, I be bebe* (dump) *wey no* fit talk to keep quiet throughout the journey? Leave me alone," Jegede reacted.

"So *Oga* said *im go* get big money, Jegede?" Johnson asked.

"Yes," he answered in a word as he was still angry with Maxwell.

"Maxwell, that is the estacode he is talking about," Johnson said and told Maxwell that the Minister's approval was in exercise of his power as provided for in Section 4(m) of the Act which says the Minister shall '*initiate, organize and participate in promotion of mineral resources development, such as conference, seminars and workshops geared towards the stimulation of investment in mineral resources.*'"

"Johnson, Austin in the Artisanal and Small Scale Mining Department told me that next week he will go to the Nigerian Institute of Mining and Geosciences (NIMG), Jos for a course on the Formation and Management of Mining Co-operative Society," Maxwell said.

143

"He should be happy. In fact, the Minister should do more on training," Johnson said.

"You are correct; one of the functions of the Minister as provided for in Section 4(g) of the Act is to build up a sound professional and technical manpower for the minerals sector which should regularly be retrained to flow with global trends," Maxwell said and kept on discussing as they go.

℘℘

After Johnson and Maxwell left for Kun, Engr. Sluice left for Danja in Katsina State. He had received a report of how alluvial gold was being mined and panned along the streams that traverse an area in the northern or north-eastern vicinity of Danja. He used the car and the driver of the Zonal Mines Officer of North Central Zone who had come to see him. When he arrived Danja, he went to request for the assistance of the Nigerian Police Force in the Divisional Police Station to provide security cover for him to go to the site as provided for in Section 122(2)(i) of the Regulations.

"I am Engr. Sluice, the Zonal Mines Officer, in-charge of North West. Is the DPO on seat?" he asked the Police Corporal at the gate.

"Yes, he is on seat. What do you want?"

"I think you should know that I am a government official. Allow me in, please," Engr. Sluice said.

"Is there anything wrong for me to ask you what you want, *Oga*?"

"Please, let me in."

The Corporal opened the gate. He went straight to the counter.

℘℘

"I am here to see the DPO. I understand he is on seat," Engr. Sluice said to a woman Sergeant at the counter,"

"*Oga,* you be soldier? *Wetin dey* make you take look serious like this? Relax now. *Im dey* but one man *dey* with him. Just wait small," the woman Corporal said and called, "Sule, take this money and go and buy *wena* from Hajiya Mero for me. Let her put two spoons of *mai shanu. Ehen, Oga,* let me tell the DPO that you are here to see him," She turned and spoke to Engr. Sluice whose face was now showing signs of impatience.

"Do you know his office," the woman Corporal asked after she returned.

"No, this is my first time of coming here," Engr. Sluice said.

"Follow me," she said and led the way. The uniform so much fitted her as if she was born with it. Many people had told her so.

"See the office there with the inscription, DPO," she pointed and returned to the counter.

ഇൻ‌ങ

As Engr. Sluice was entering the DPO's office, the man who was with the DPO was coming out. They met at the door.

"Good Morning," Engr. Sluice greeted the man as he was passing him.

"Good Morning, Chairman," the man responded without stopping. He was fond of nicknaming people with signs of decency like that. Both of them seemed to be in a hurry.

ഇൻ‌ങ

"Good morning, DPO. I am Engr. Sluice, the Zonal Mines Officer for North West Zone."

"You are very much welcome. I am Umar Kebbok. What can I do for you?"

"I am here to request for security cover to the site where they are mining gold. They are illegal miners. One boy who will lead me to the site is in the vehicle, waiting."

"As a matter of fact, I have heard about that. I want to settle down before I will go there. I was just posted here three days ago."

"Three days ago?"

"Yes, I am a new person here. Engr., I will assist you but we have a problem of fuel shortage. The tank of the Police vehicle is almost empty. You will have to find some money to buy fuel."

"You want me to fuel the car as a government official? Where do you think I will get the money? You Police get problem."

"Your office *dey* give *una* sufficient money like before? Answer me. We just *dey* manage to do our work. It has not been easy, you know."

"Everywhere is like that. Will three thousand naira do?"

"Make it five thousand naira."

"You are asking for five thousand naira?"

"That is correct."

"DPO, I know you're teasing me!"

"I am not; unless you don't want the security cover anymore."

In pains, Engr. Sluice squeezed out the five thousand naira and gave to him. He wondered how government wanted good work performance without adequate logistics support.

A team of the Police was organized and they left for the site.

ഇൻൽ

"This is the road to the site," the boy that was directing Engr. Sluice said as they got to an off-set that leads to the site. It was about 1.5 kilometers off the main road which is also an off-set from Hunkuyi - Danja road, leading to Kankara.

"Park the vehicle here," the boy said. If we get close to them with the vehicle they will hear the sound and run away. They normally have watchmen. We will have to trek a distance of about 600 metres to the site."

"No problem, we can do that," Engr. Sluice said, buckling up his boots.

"Let us go, gentlemen," he said after he had finished.

As they approached the site, they saw a boy who quickly ran back to the site, blowing a whistle that sounded *gu-du, gu-du, gu-du* (run-away, run-away, run-away). That was the notification sound of danger coming to the illegal miners.

The illegal mining site was a depression that edged with a lovely to behold stretch of plain land to the west with dotted settlements typical of village setting. The contact of the eastern edge of the depression is a stretch of land that gently slopes towards the road leading to Kankara. When Engr. Sluice and the rest got to the eastern edge of the depression, they saw many people running in different directions, leaving their work implements and motor cycles. Unfortunately, one old man who could not run away because he was a cripple was arrested.

147

"Who asked you to come and mine gold here illegally?" Engr. Sluice asked the old man.

"We *dey* mine the gold for Alhaji Mubarak."

"Where is he?"

"See him *for* those shrubs over there. He is hiding there, "Alhaji Mubarak was the man who was leaving the DPO's office as Engr. Sluice was entering.

"Corporals, go and arrest the man and bring him here," Engr. Sluice ordered.

Alhaji Mubarak heard them and began to run but he was too heavy to run far.

"Stop there!" the Corporals shouted, running after him. He removed his gown and tried to jump across a stream but he fell in and wounded his knees on the pebbles in the stream. He could not stand up to continue escaping. He was caught.

"Alhaji Mubarak, are you the guilty person?" the Police Corporals asked in shock and wished he had not done that. They had just exchanged courtesies with him in the office. He had been generous to them. Now they know the money was from here, the illegal gold mining operation. But what can they do? They are not alone. They have to lead him to Engr. Sluice for interrogation.

ℴℙ

"*Ehen, no be* you I just met in the office of the DPO? So you are the one sponsoring this illegal mining. Alhaji, why are you doing this? You will face the law," Engr. Sluice fumed and told the Police to handcuff him and the crippled old man. He also asked them to pick the work implements and motorcycles at the site as hard evidences against them. The owners of the motorcycles will have to go to the Police Station for their motorcycles or risk losing them. The DPO will equally be surprised to see Alhaji Mubarak who had visited his office that day being presented to him as a culprit. Engr. Sluice had vowed to allow the law takes its course without listening to any plea from anybody….

ဢဢ

"Jegede, stop the car. Kun is not too far anymore. We will soon be there. Let me speak to the Civil Defence Corps. Maxwell, we have to strategize on how to handle the situation. Alight from the car and let us see them together," Johnson said.

"Inspector of the Corps (IC), we are almost getting to Kun, the place of our mission. I want you people to handle the situation with all seriousness. Do you have any advice for us?"

"We don't have any advice. We will do only what you tell us."

"Okay, let's go. Maxwell, let us go. Jegede, move on," Johnson said and the Civil Defence Corps followed.

"See the place over there. There are many dump trucks there today. The excavator is working. Increase the speed, Jegede," Johnson said.

"If I speed, you will complain. I am tired of your confusion." Jegede Complained.

"Keep quiet!" Johnson shouted at Jegede. "Maxwell, get your camera set. You know we have to produce digital pictures of the site and the machinery. You must also take the pictures of the leaders of this illegal activity."

ဢဢ

"You guys," the Inspector of the Corps began, "don't make a mistake and shoot anybody. We are to arrest for the law to take its course," he said to his men as they drove on.

"Yes, sir," they answered.

As they approached the site, they saw one black jeep going to the site ahead of them. The jeep was parking as they reached the site.

"All work must stop! Who is your leader here?" Johnson spoke. The Security and Civil Defence Corps were combat ready to obviate any resistance.

"Alhaji Hashimu Kun," a man with a black polythene bag said.

"And you, who are you?" Johnson kept on asking.

"I am the supervisor,"

"By the way, where is Alhaji Kun?"

"See him inside the jeep."

"Inspector, the principal culprit is in the jeep. Let us see him. Let your men stay behind and make sure nobody escapes. Maxwell, stay with them. Remember, the digital pictures. Take as many as you can. Capture every necessary detail. They will be used as evidences against them. After all, to the Minister, report on illegal mining activities is not complete without pictorial evidence. I don't have to tell you this. You know it. Inspector, let us go and see the man in the jeep."

"Are you the person working illegally here? Why did you choose to do this?"

"What do you mean? I say what do you mean? You, you mean I should not work in my land? This land that is my inheritance from my ancestors! You are joking," Alhaji Kun flared up.

150

"*Heh*, who are you? What do you want here," a hefty man of mass muscles, who was wearing dark goggles as if he were an actor, came out of the jeep and asked. A second person more intimidating than him also came out from the jeep, taking majestic steps towards the Inspector of Corps and asked, "Are you here to cause confusion? Do you think you can intimidate us? You don't know anything yet. We will deal with you, now. Master," referring to Alhaji Kun, "allow us to do our work."

"Karfe, don't do anything yet. I want to understand who they are. Did you hear me?" Alhaji Kun said.

"Alhaji, we know it is your land. But Section 1 of the Act says the control of all mineral resources in any land in Nigeria is vested in the Government of the Federation and they shall only be given to people who are interested to mine in accordance with the provisions of the Act. Whether the mineral is found in your bedroom, you have no right to mine it in contravention of the Act," Johnson explained.

"You are joking, my friend! What Act?" Alhaji Kun continued to flare up.

"You are under arrest," the Inspector of the Corps said and fired into the air. The two hefty men ran back into the jeep. "Nobody should misbehave. I am not joking." The Inspector called on two of his corps members. They came and handcuffed Alhaji Kun and the two hefty men. Some other arrests of key people and vehicles were made. They were taken to a police station to be treated in accordance with the relevant laws....

ഇന്റ

"You guys are welcome. You have done a good job. I have just been phoned from the office of the Governor that they are interested in this case for political reasons but the law must take its course. I assure you. I will resist political and favouritism games in this case. Wait and see," Engr. Sluice said as he finished hearing from Johnson and Maxwell before they would submit a written report on the matter to him.

TEN

Before Engr. Sluice got to the office in the morning one day, a group of people from a growing mining community had earlier arrived that morning and were waiting for him. They had come to protest against an established gold mining company which they thought had polluted their only source of clean water by the use of mining chemicals to leach the gold from the ores, thereby violating the provisions of Section 174 of the Regulations on social concerns for mining communities.

"Who are those people standing at the door of my office?" Engr. Sluice asked no one in particular. He was talking to himself as they drove into the office yard.

"If you get to your office you will know, sir," Alice said. When going to the office that morning, Engr. Sluice had given her a lift while passing through her area of residence where he had gone to see somebody, his tribal man, to woo him into the Mining industry.

"I hope there is no problem, Jegede," he said. "Stop, Jegede; see Johnson over there. What is he checking for in the rubbish? Alice, go and call him for me. Let me find out from him who those people are. These days, bad people are all over the place. One has to be careful."

"*Oga*, you too *dey* fear," Jegede said. "Nobody will kidnap you," he added.

"Shut up!" Engr. Sluice shouted at him and looked at him as if he would fling him out of the vehicle and suddenly turned to ask Johnson who had come, "Who are the people at the door of my office?"

"It is the Chief of Malamko with his people."

"Mallam Auta?" he asked

"Yes, sir."

"Jegede, let us go," he said, feeling safe as he knew Mallam Auta very well. He was a man of peace. He hated any form of violence.

"Chief, why are you here this early morning? I hope there is no problem," Engr. Sluice asked as he alighted from the vehicle.

"Big problem, sir," one of the people that came with the Chief said.

"*Yi shuru* (keep quiet)," the Chief said to the man. "Inspector, enter your office first. We will talk."

"Okay, Chief," he responded and entered the office, leaving them outside. While he was entering his office, he sent for Johnson. "Alice, call Johnson for me. I want him to treat one letter now-now."

Johnson was already at the door, coming to see him on some issues.

"*Yauwa* (That is good), *Oga* wants to see you."

"Johnson, this is a letter from Senator Bisi, requesting me to defer the payment of royalty on the Kyanite he is mining. I don't have the statutory power to do so. It is only the Minister that can do that for a certain period subject to the approval of the Federal Executive Council (FEC) as provided for in Section 33(3) of the Act. Go and draft a reply to the letter and ask him to address the letter to the Minister if he is still interested. As you go out, tell the Chief and his people to come in quickly. I will be going to Birnin Gwari this morning."

"Chief, *Oga* said you should go in," Johnson related the message. They went in.

154

"Chief, how are you doing?" Engr. Sluice asked, holding a copy of the programme of a one day interactive stakeholders meeting with the Federal Mines Officers and the Technical Departments of the Ministry graciously organized by the Director-General, Mining Cadastre Office under the theme. '*Strengthening The Existing Synergy Between Mining Cadastre Office And The Technical Departments For Enhanced Mineral Title Administration And Effective Regulations Of The Mining Industry Operations.*' He felt bad as many mineral title holders still find it difficult to document their mineral titles in the Mines Offices in compliance with one of the resolutions arrived at that meeting held at Rockview Royale Hotel, Wuse II, Abuja. He kept aside the copy of the programme to listen to Mallam Auta, the Chief.

"I am doing fine, Inspector *na mu* (our inspector)."

"Tell me the reason for coming here this early morning. Is there any problem, Chief?"

"Inspector Sluice, we have a problem. Increase Gross Domestic Product Limited is spoiling the only source of clean water we have in the village. My people are no longer safe. Many frogs and fishes are dying in the river we drink from. I am worried that people will soon start dying just like the frogs and the fishes."

"Inspector, we will chase away the company from our community," one of the men spoke in anger, hitting the table of Engr. Sluice as if he was the person doing the mining in their community.

"Yes, we are silently dying. Mr. Kent has to leave our community if he will not stop polluting the only source of clean water we have," another man spoke.

"Not only that! Some of the miners are marrying our women. An abomination! They are doing this because they have the money. One week ago, Danliti lost his wife to a miner who immediately resigned from the company thereafter. We learnt they have gone to Cameroon. The man is from there," another man fumed.

"Calm down, my people; let us talk gently. I know we are in pain. I know this but we should be patient. Anger is not the solution to all this," the Chief intervened. As they were talking, they heard the sound of a vehicle being parked outside Engr. Sluice's office. It was Mr. Kent that had come. He had been told by an informant about the Chief and his people coming to see Engr. Sluice that morning. He entered the office.

"See the man that is killing us! Inspector, this man will leave our community. We can't continue to allow him to pollute our river. He must leave," a fierce looking man who had not spoken since they entered Engr. Sluice's office stood up and said, pointing a finger at Mr. Kent.

"You people should remember that you are in my office. You must listen to your Chief and behave well. I can't take this from you anymore. You must respect this office," Engr. Sluice showed his displeasure and turned to Mr. Kent and said, "You are welcome; you came at the right time. Sit down, please. Do you have any other thing to say, Chief?"

"That is our major problem, Inspector. We thank God that Mr. Kent is here by providence," he said not knowing that one of his trusted persons was an informant to Mr. Kent about anything that is discussed concerning him in the village.

"Mr. Kent, the Chief and his people are accusing you of polluting their only source of clean water by the use of mining chemicals in the processing of the gold. They are also accusing your workers of marrying their women. What do you have to say about these serious accusations?"

"I don't use mining chemicals in processing the gold. I am innocent of what they are accusing me of. It is illegal miners that use mining chemicals like mercury to process the gold in their streams. Concerning the marrying of their women, my employees can't do that. We are friendly to any of our host communities anywhere we go. The Cameroonian they said ran away with one of their wives was not my worker. He was one of the illegal miners. The Chief, through a surrogate, is conniving with the illegal miners to work in the night in my Mining Lease area. Silently, not wanting to publically disgrace him, I have been pleading with him to stop that but he would not listen."

"Chief! Chief! Did you hear what Mr. Kent said? Is that correct?" one of the people spoke. He was one of the people the Chief was trying to woo for support in running the village because he commanded a lot of respect in the village and could make it difficult for him to rule. He was stubbornly courageous anywhere he went.

"Maikudi, *ka kwanta da zuciyarka* (you should calm down your mind). *Za mu yi maganar in mu koma gida* (we will discuss when we get back home)," the Chief pleaded, having no more courage to speak. He knew Mr. Kent had sufficient evidence to disgrace him.

"What did he say?" Engr. Sluice asked the people.

"Forget, sir," Maikudi said, not wanting to disgrace their Chief. No matter what, he respected the chieftaincy stool of his village even if the person occupying it misbehaved or was not worthy. He was that honourable.

"Now, all of you have heard Mr. Kent. Do you have any objection to what he said?" Engr. Sluice asked. Not wanting to embarrass the king on the allegation in their presence, he decided he would see him at a later day.

"For now, leave the matter as it is. We will return home to investigate the allegation Mr. Kent has made against the Chief. Thank you, Inspector; we are going now. Chief, stand up and let us go," Maikudi said and began to go out. The Chief and the others followed, returning home in a mood similar to that of defeated warriors returning from war. Their enemy, Mr. Kent, seemed to have defeated them unless the proposed investigation proved otherwise.

"Mr. Kent, are you not going with them?"

"Inspector, why did you ask me this kind of question? You and I have not seen for two months now. There is need for me to stay behind to discuss some issues with you. After all, I did not come together with them."

"You are right. Mr. Kent, I can see how troublesome these people can be."

"They are always troublesome. They are difficult people to live with. I can't just understand why they are acting like this."

"My advice to you is that you should comply with the provisions of Section 174 of the Regulations on social concerns for mining communities, especially in the area of identifying and accessing '*options for avoiding, mitigating, or compensating groups which may be adversely affected* as stipulated in sub-section 3(b) of Section 174 of the Regulations. Do that so as to be at peace with the community for the success of your project."

"You are correct, Inspector. For your information, the Mines Environmental Compliance Department, in exercising her duty as provided in Section 175 of the Regulations, has approved my proposed Environmental Protection and Rehabilitation Programme. I am happy about that."

"That is good information. Congrats. Are you complying with the provision of Section 176(1) of the Regulations by contributing to the Environmental Protection and Rehabilitation Fund?"

"Inspector, the Mines Environmental Compliance Department and my company have determined the amount for us to contribute to the Fund. I have started paying the contribution in compliance with Section 175(6) of the Regulations. You know I don't play with issues that can damage the reputation of my company."

"I know. These villagers are yet to know who you are."

"Just forget about them. I know they will go and fight the Chief because of what I said."

"You are welcome. I should be on my way to Birnin Gwari now."

That is alright, Inspector; till next time."

ഇൽ

Engr. Russo Sluice and Jegede, his sanguine driver, had gone far from the office on their way to take samples of Kyanite from a hill in Birnin Gwari, Kaduna state, when their vehicle developed a

159

mechanical fault. Jegede parked the vehicle by the road side to check what the problem could be.

"*Oga*," Jegede called, "*e be* like *say* there is a problem," he said, lying under the vehicle.

"What is the problem?" Engr. Sluice asked, looking disappointed. He was working on time so as to return to the office in good time for a scheduled appointment.

"Let me check *am* again. I *wan* be sure," Jegede said. Engr. Sluice kept quiet.

"*Oga*, give me the jack. *E be like say* I *go jeck* (jack) up the motor to check well-well." Engr. Sluice removed it from the booth and gave it to him.

"*Oga*, give me that stone," Jegede said, pointing at the stone, "the *jeck* (jack) *dey go* down-down because the ground is soft. I want to put *am* on the stone so that e *go standeh solid*," Engr. Sluice went for the stone.

"Thank you, sir," he thanked, laughing within himself how he was instructing Engr. Sluice, his boss. He lay under the vehicle, checking it, saying it could be a big problem.

"What exactly is the problem, Jegede?" Engr. Sluice asked, becoming more restless.

"I am still checking *am*, sir; bring the bags of the spanners to me quickly," he told Engr. Sluice.

"You are just sending me without fear. Don't you respect me as your *Oga*?"

Jegede laughed.

"Why are you laughing?"

"You *no* know about situational leadership? In this present situation, I *be* the cool leader for that matter. Sir, I *dey* always respect you but in this situation how you *go* expect me to be coming every time from under the vehicle to take anything I want?

You *go* help me so that we *go* be fast. I am the Situational Leader now. After I repair the vehicle, I *go* reverse to my position."

Engr. Sluice smiled and shook his head. He decided in his mind what he would do to curtail the excesses of Jegede. However, he knew it was necessary for a good and an unhindered communication environment to exist between a leader and all strata of his subordinates to enhance job performance. He had a vision of creating an environment of a family in the workplace so as to unite the workers to work as a team.

"*Oga, e be* like *say* you *go* call a mechanic to come and repair this vehicle. I *no* understand *wetin be d* matter with *tam.*"

"And you claimed to be a driver-mechanic? I will change your position to that of an ordinary driver," Engr. Sluice threatened. Jegede saw the seriousness and the anger in him and he was wise to keep quiet. He knew that when the animal side of Sluice has been aroused, anything could happen…

Engr. Sluice decided to call his mechanic from Kaduna.

ഇരുട്ട

"Baba Kekere, do you know Udawa along Kaduna – Birnin Gwari road?" Engr. Sluice called the mechanic through his mobile phone.

"Udawa, Udawa; yes, I know Udawa! What is the problem, sir?"

"Leave everything you are doing now and set out for Udawa with your working tools. My vehicle has a problem. When you pass the village about two kilometers, you will see us. No delay please."

"Okay, sir; I will be coming right away."

"Who has spoken to you, Baba Kekere?" a man, Mr. Uduak, who had brought his car for repair, asked.

"*Na* Inspector for mining matters."

"Is it Engr. Sluice?"

"*Na im*; you know *am*?"

"Yes; I have an appointment with him today at 3pm. As a matter of fact, I want my car to be fixed so that I use it to go for the appointment. Where is he now?"

"Udawa."

"Udawa! That is far. How can you repair my car, now?

"I have solved the major problem. My colleague, Lai, will complete the job; Lai, complete this job; no mistake, please," Baba Kekere instructed and left for Udawa.

While Engr. Sluice was waiting for the arrival of Baba Kekere, the Managing Director of a mining company, Ambassador Jimada, was on his way from Birnin Gwari to see him in Kaduna on the issue of the revocation of his mineral title and to initiate a Memorandum of Understanding with one mining company based in Kaduna on exchange of knowledge, data management and co-operation on technical matters. On approaching Udawa, he saw Engr. Sluice by the road side and stopped.

"Inspector, what is the problem that you are standing in this dangerous place? This is a regular operational point of armed robbers. Don't you see the big stones over there? They use them to block the road anytime they operate. Last week I nearly ran into them while they were operating here. I arrived here after 30 minutes of the operation."

"I know about this place but what can I do. We can't carry the vehicle on our heads. It has broken down and we are waiting for a mechanic who is coming from Kaduna."

"You can leave your driver here to wait for him. You can go back with me to Kaduna. Will that be okay with you? I have some discussion with you if we get to your office."

"How can I leave my driver here alone especially in this dangerous place? I must not do this, Ambassador. The mechanic will soon be here," he said. Engr. Sluice was a man who would not be at peace with himself to abandon any of his subordinates in times of uncertainty. He would always be there for them as he knew that will increase their loyalty to him apart from moral consideration.

"No problem, Inspector. As a matter of fact, what I want to discuss with you is on the revocation of my mineral title by the Mining Cadastre Office without giving me notice. That is very wrong."

"Wait, Ambassador. I know when you got the title you are talking about, your office was not in the present address. Did you notify the Mining Cadastre Office of your change of address in compliance with Section 104 of the Regulations?"

"I did not."

"*Ehen*, this is where the problem lies. Notices were sent to the last known addresses of defaulters in Nigeria for them to remedy their defaults. How did I know this? I was a co-opted member of the Committee that carried out the recent exercise of revocation."

"Is that so?"

"Yes; the Registry Department of the Mining Cadastre Office sent letters to the last known addresses of defaulters in accordance with the provisions of Section 151(3) of the Act for them to remedy the defaults within 30 days in compliance with Section 97(3)(a) of the Regulations. According to the Act, that was '*sufficient notice of the revocation of the mineral title to the mineral title holder.*' This is very clear, Ambassador. The mistake was yours because you did not notify the MCO of your change of address."

"What can I do now to have my site back?"

"Ambassador, you may wish to come to my office on appointment to be guided properly. I am not in the mood now to begin to advise you on what to do," Engr. Sluice said. Until the vehicle is repaired, he does not think he can concentrate on any other thing and discuss it to his satisfaction.

"*Oga, Oga*, see people in the bush running towards us! They have guns! Let us run, sir!" Jegede shouted in fear.

"Ambassador, armed robbers, armed bandits; let us run, runnnn, Jegede," Engr. Sluice said in anxiety especially as they had just discussed on the danger of the area in terms of armed robbery.

"Yahuza, come out of the vehicle; armed robbers!" Ambassador Jimada shouted at his driver.

The four of them ran towards Udawa. While running, the Ambassador fell down as he was entangled by the *baban riga* (the flowing gown) he wore. He removed and left it behind. A man who was fetching firewood close by saw them running and asked them why they were running.

"Why are you running? *Heh*, I am asking you people!"

"Armed robbers!" Ambassador Jimada said, wondering how Engr. Sluice could run faster than all of them. Engr. Sluice jogs every two days apart from walking in the bush for many hours during field inspections and sometimes while carrying out contracted surveys on weekend days. He was so patriotic not to use government time for his personal interest.

The man fetching the firewood discovered that the supposed armed robbers were actually local hunters from his village, running after an animal one of them had shot and he shouted, "*Heh*, stop running! They are hunters! I say stop running! They are hunters!"

Yahuza, the driver to Ambassador Jimada, was running behind his boss. He heard the man very well and stopped to look at the direction the supposed armed robbers were coming from. He saw they were running back towards where they came. They were trailing the animal they had shot.

"*Oga*, they are not armed robbers, stop running!" Yahuza shouted. Ambassador Jimada turned and looked back. Indeed, the supposed armed robbers were running towards a different direction. Engr. Sluice ran to a seemingly safe distance before he stopped. He saw Ambassador Jimada and Yahuza standing and the man with the firewood going to them. Jegede reached where he was standing.

"*Oga*, when we go back I *go* tell Johnson, Maxwell and Alice how you *come tear* race passed everybody. Life is sweet oh. *Na wa, Oga*. You even run pass Ambassador who is younger than you. I know *say* you senior *am*."

"Shut up, *yeye* man. Who *wan* die?"

Jegede laughed and laughed and bent down to hold his stomach and said '*chai*', wonders *no go* end *lai -lai*."

"Will you keep quiet or not?" Engr. Sluice said and began to go back to where Ambassador Jimada, Yahuza and the man with the firewood were standing.

"Inspector Sluice, you are a good material for a track event. See how you ran pass all of us! I am surprised," Ambassador Jimada said. Engr. Sluice ignored him.

"Yes this place is not a good place to stop. Armed robbers always operate at this place. Last year, in this very place, they operated and collected large quantities of gold from the people coming from Tsohon Birnin Gwari. Some of the miners are informants to the armed robbers. We in this village have no peace because of this evil. We don't know what to do now," the man with the fire wood said and hissed pathetically.

As they were still talking, a vehicle came and stopped abruptly before them. Engr. Sluice and Ambassador Jimada appeared to want to run, thinking the people in the vehicle were armed robbers. They were not. Baba Kekere was in the vehicle.

೩೦೧೩

"Baba Kekere; I *dey* happy now as you *don* come!" Jegede rejoiced.

"Where is the vehicle and what is the problem?" Baba Kekere asked.

"See *am* there. It *dey* make one bad noise and *e no dey* move fast as before. I *don* understand *wetin* be *e* problem."

166

Nobody told Baba Kekere about what had just happened to them so that he would be in a relaxed mood to repair the vehicle. They went to where the vehicle was.

"Start *am* (the vehicle) and let me hear how e *dey* sound," Baba Kekere told Jegede. He did. Baba Kekere could not really understand what the mechanical fault was. He decided to test run it by himself to a distance and toward Birnin Gwari. While he was going, he saw the hunters with the animal they were chasing, he bought it from them.

ℰᴑᴼᴿ

Engr. Sluice and others kept on discussing, waiting for Baba Kekere to return.

"Inspector, I applied in good time for the renewal of my Exploration Licence in Jigawa State but up to now I have not heard from the Mining Cadastre Office and the Licence has expired. What do you think will happen?" Ambassador Jimada asked.

"Since you have applied in good time you don't have any problem to continue with your exploration activities until the MCO takes a decision, favourable or unfavourable, on it as provided in Section 39(2) of the Regulations. So, carry on with your exploration activities as if nothing has happened."

"I am happy to hear this from you. I was already afraid that my technical partners from Chile who knew the Licence has expired would not like to continue with the work. They had told me that they do not want to work with an expired mineral title."

"If they doubt what I have told you, bring them to my office for me to explain to them. They know little about our mining laws."

"Okay, Inspector."

Baba Kekere returned and told them he knew what the problem with the vehicle was. He fixed the vehicle within a short time.

"Ambassador, my vehicle has been fixed. I am going back to Kaduna for an appointment."

"*Ehen, Oga*, the time you called me to come, I *dey* with one man called Uduak. *Im* came to my workshop to repair *im* vehicle. *Im* told me *say e* get appointment with you today. I *don go* far-far with *im* job but I leave *am* quick-quick to come and meet *una. Na* Lai *dey* complete *im* work."

"Yes, that is the man I will be keeping an appointment with. He is an old miner who knows what he is doing."

"So *im* be good man. Speak well-well about me to the man so that *im go* keep take *en* car come to my workshop for repair if *e* get problem."

"Don't worry, I will do that. Ambassador, I am going now. Are you still going to Kaduna?"

"No, maybe, I will come tomorrow. I am not sure. Yahuza, we too can start going," he said and gave the man with the fire wood some money. There was nothing that gave him joy more than touching the lives of people positively.

They parted ways. They left the man with the fire wood and he returned to the village with unspeakable joy. But Engr. Sluice's appointment with Mr. Uduak would never take place that day. As soon as Baba Kekere left for Udawa to attend to Engr. Sluice, Mr. Uduak was called by his Mines Manager to go to the mine immediately to settle a problem between his company and the host community. He had to hire a vehicle and immediately left because his own was still under repair. Engr. Sluice would only discover that when he returned. In anxiety, Mr. Uduak forgot to call and tell him that he would no longer be able to keep the appointment. They would reschedule it for another day because it was very important for them to meet.

ELEVEN

"Mr. Uduak, before you come here to do your mining, we have been using this road, our great grandfathers even used this road. You can't stop us from using this road to our farms," Dantsoho, the youths leader of Gidan Mutum Daya, where the mineral title of Mr. Uduak was, said. He was at the site with many of the village youths.

"It would be a taboo for somebody to say our feet will not match where the blessed feet of our forefathers had matched; never! I say never! Ya yi Kadan ya hana mu bi. wannan hanya. Wane shi? (He is too small to prevent us from using the road. Who is he)?" a well-muscled youth of medium height said and told some youths to uproot the obstruction Mr. Uduak had put across the road to prevent the villagers from passing through the area of the subject of his mineral title. They instantly did.

"Everybody should pass to the farm; let me see the person who will stop you. People from the town think we are fools. Everywhere people are now aware of their human rights," the well-muscled youth said. The people who were many in number, and some who had their dogs with them, began to pass to their farms.

"Ibrahim," Mr. Uduak called the well-muscled youth who was telling the people to pass, "don't you know what you are doing is wrong? I will report you people to the Police," he said and told his Mines Manager, Engr. Solomon Kasuwa, who was with him to go and call the mine workers to come and reinstate the obstruction.

"Sir, just leave that for now," Engr. Solomon Kasuwa said. He knew if he did that there would be violence which could lead to the loss of lives. The anger of the people had been bottled up for long and would no longer be contained. It could burst out like new wine in an old skin.

"Go and call them. We will be here waiting for you. Today we will know who owns the land. We will know who the heavens will take sides with. Go and come," Ibrahim spoke, beating his chest and pacing around, looking as fierce as a mad person who was ready to do anything. His eyes appeared as if tongues of fire would come out of them.

"This man wants to test our will. He thinks we are stupid people," a youth from the militant group surged towards Mr. Uduak and spoke in anger. He was only short of releasing the demons in him to deal with Mr. Uduak who was visibly in shock and terrified.

As they were quarrelling, the Chief of the village, Mallam Danyaro, who had been informed about what was happening, came.

"Dantsoho, I told you to follow this thing gently. Why are you here to fight this man after I have assured you that I will talk with him on this matter? Anything that happens here I will be blamed and the village will suffer for it.

Where are some of the youths of Garin Zinariya today? I ask all of you; where are they today? Do you want what happened there to happen in this village? I can't allow this. This will only happen after my death. Don't you know the importance of a visitor in our midst especially this man from the South? Even if he is wrong, we should follow the rule of law to demand for justice."

171

But …," Ibrahim wanted to say something.

"Don't say anything; I am not ready to listen to any of you now. All of you should go back home. Mr. Uduak, don't do anything that will further escalate this problem," the Chief spoke and started his motorcycle and went back. He did not come with his low-suspended car. The road was not good. It had many stumps and potholes.

The youths grumbled and returned home. Mallam Danyaro knew how to use authority with diplomacy. The youths respected him unlike the youths of Garin Zinariya who disrespected their chief and beat the Mines Manager of a mining company which had violated Section 114(c) of the Regulations on the obligations of Mining Lease and Quarry Lease holder by not complying with some obligations contained in the Community Development Agreement (CDA) it had agreed with the community. One of such violated agreements was that of employment mix of unskilled labour force. The company did not reflect a favourable community content as initially agreed and unambiguously contained in the CDA. That was what angered the youths of Garin Zinariya. Unfortunately, they took the law into their hands instead of following the healthy channels of rule of law by beating the Mines Manager. This caused his right leg to fracture. The youths of Garin Zinariya were arrested and detained with huge financial, social and psychological consequences. Mallam Danyaro would not allow such a nasty experience in his jurisdiction. He had resolved in his mind since that day to call for a meeting of the whole village on the issue and to go with Mr. Uduak to see Engr. Russo Sluice, the Inspector of Mines, on how the issue would be resolved.... As this was going on, Engr. Sluice was settling a boundary dispute between two mining co-operatives somewhere.

ℬℭ

"Mr. Dantoro, why do you continue to encroach into the Small Scale Mining Lease area of Poverty Reduction Mining Co-operative?" Engr. Sluice, the Inspector of Mines, asked. Dantoro was the Chairman of Eating Through Mining Co-operative. His wife and all his children, four of them, were members of the co-operative. His first son was the Secretary of the Co-operative while his third son, Dan-mutum, was the treasurer. In the meetings of the co-operative, he and his family dominated the deliberations to the chagrin of the others.

"Master," Dan-mutum wanted to speak. He called Engr. Sluice master because that was how his colleagues and himself addressed the Chinese in a Green Tourmaline mine somewhere in the South where he previously worked as if they were unconsciously recalling the days of slavery when master-slave relationship existed under an environment of inhumanity.

"Call me Engr. Sluice and not master. Are you a slave or a servant to me? I am not your master. You are reminding me of a nasty epoch in the history of mankind, slavery. I asked your father and you wanted to talk. Has he asked you to be his mouth piece? Do you think this is a small matter? You young men think you know better. That is why you always make mistake here and there. Now, Dantoro, tell me why do you keep doing this after the Director-General of the Mining Cadastre Office had resolved this matter and written to you on the resolution in compliance with Section 109(1) of the Regulations?"

173

"Inspector, you know I have not really agreed on how this dispute was resolved. I told the Director of Concessions that I was not satisfied with the resolution on this dispute and you know this since we went to Abuja together."

"And you decided to take the law into your hands, isn't it?"

"What do you want me to do, Inspector?"

"You should have appealed to the Honourable Minister as provided for in sub-section 3 of Regulation 109 if you were not satisfied with the resolution reached by the Director-General within a period of 30 days from the date of the receipt of the notice of the resolution. You still have 3 days left for you to make the appeal. But I know it will be a futile exercise as I believe the Director-General and the Director of Concessions have thoroughly and justly done their work on this matter."

"I will take the matter to court. Who is he to keep on disturbing people," Comrade Anas, the Chairman of Poverty Reduction Mining Co-operative spoke.

"That is exactly what we are going to do; the cheating is too much," the Secretary of Poverty Reduction Mining Co-operative said and told Engr. Sluice, "leave us with him; we can drag this case to anywhere. He is doing all this because there is little of the sapphire vein in their Lease. It is our luck to have much of the sapphire vein in ours. They should go and find a better place instead of wasting their time here."

"Matthew, stop talking nonsense! Are you the one to tell us what to do? What do you know about mining? As the Secretary of your co-operative, you are just stealing their money. I will make sure they remove you from that seat," Dan-mutum reacted and

174

caused an all-round quarrel. He removed a demarcation marker of a close by boundary line in annoyance to the anger of Engr. Sluice.

"Dan-mutum, stop that arrogance! I am warning you to stop what you are doing. You have contravened the provisions of Section 137 of the Act by willfully interfering with a boundary mark. It is an offence. The law will catch up with you. I will make sure you pay the fine of ₦500,000:00 or be imprisoned for not less than 2 years or be subjected to both as prescribed in Section 138(2)(a) of the Act. Wait and see," Engr. Sluice said while the Chairmen of the two co-operatives were at each others' necks, and so were their members. It was a pathetic and shameful scene contrary to the desire of the Ministry of Mines and Steel Development for an orderly, friendly and an enabling mining environment to exist in all mines fields. Eat Through Mining Co-operative would be penalized in accordance with the provisions of the mining law to serve as a deterrent to others. Sanity must be restored to the mines fields. Engr. Sluice resolved. He immediately ordered the two mining co-operatives to stop work pending further resolution of the dispute.

The Minister had recently ordered for the restoration of sanity in the mines fields while having a consultative meeting with the Agencies and the Departmental heads of the Ministry. It was at that meeting that the Director, Mines Environmental Compliance Department (MEC), said that he was doing his best to make mining companies comply with the prescription of Section 182 of the Regulations by filing annual reclamation statements. In addition, he said he was trying to have other companies comply with the prescription of Section 180 of the

Regulations by submitting for approval an amended reclamation plan necessitated by '*changes in product prices, economics, financing unanticipated conditions, or suspension of mining operations... before modifying the approval reclamation work.*'

The Director of Mines Environmental Compliance Department (MEC) further briefed that his department was not satisfied with the report of one company on procedure intended to be followed before dumping her mine waste which was not based strictly on Section 192 of the Regulations and had directed the company to comply with the provisions of sub-section 3 of the Regulation 192 by conducting '*additional survey tests, borehole or ground-water measurements.*' He concluded by saying his Department was always ensuring that mineral title holders stated '*the safety precaution and the other measures to be taken to protect the environment surrounding the,*' waste, '*dumping areas, before dumping any material on that site*' in compliance with the provision of Section 192(2) of the Regulations.

On his own part, the Director of Artisanal and Small Scale Mining Department said the leadership of the Miners' Association of Nigeria had been disturbing him on when the extension services would be provided for its teaming members all over the country. On this note, the Minister, who was so concerned about repositioning the informal miners under a robust regulatory framework, said the problem of miners would be over as soon as the Solid Minerals Development Fund became operational. However, he cautioned that only serious and compliant miners would be considered for extension services.

The Director of Concessions who represented the Director-General of the Mining Cadastre Office who had gone to South Africa to deliver a paper on *"The Cadastral Form Of Administration Of Mineral Titles:- The Teething Problems And How Far We Have Overcome Some Of Them"* said a list of defaulting mineral titles was being compiled to seek the Minister's approval for their revocation. He further said the management of the Mining Cadastre Office could presently and favourably compete in terms of expertise with any other in the world. On this, the Minister said he knew how serious they were and promised to make available resources for them to succeed. The Minister was applauded.

The Director of Mines Inspectorate Department who had just returned yesterday from an international seminar on the rising prices of mineral commodities in Chile said that quarry operators, especially the minors, were finding it challenging to operate their quarries because of the difficulty to access explosives. He wished the Minister might consider how the quarry operators could be helped as their businesses were dying.... He was only short of requesting the Minister to kindly consider allowing the Federal Mines Officers (FMOs) to carefully approve applications for the purchase and immediate use of commercial explosives and accessories by small scale operators in the mining industry under the strict and collaborative supervision by Mines Officers and the staff of relevant security agencies, so as to alleviate their problem of accessing the blasting materials, pending the total restoration of the former procedural structure of dealing with issues of explosives to the FMOs when the security challenges confronting the peace of the nation are contained. To avoid being misunderstood, and that was his fear, he decided to be quiet on that though he was pained by the lack of revenue in royalty from such operators.

At the end of the consultative meeting, the Minister told them that the Federal Executive Council had approved the formation of the National Council on Mining and Mineral Resources Development (NCMMRD). From the faces of the Minister, the Minister of State and the Permanent Secretary, one could see carpets of joy spread all over. They were only humble enough not to say it out that the NCMMRD was formed during their time in office. Everybody will feel that way.

"The NCMMRD is a platform for stakeholders in the mining industry to meet annually and discuss the progress and the challenges of the mining industry and make recommendations that may be adopted by the government in making policy instruments to move it forward," the Minister of State was heard telling his counterpart from another Ministry who had just arrived immediately after the closure of the consultative meeting. He also told him that he would soon go with the Minister to London in the United Kingdom to attend Mines and Money Conference.

It was after that consultative meeting that the Director of Mines Inspectorate instructed all the Zonal Mines Officers and the Federal Mines Officers to sanitize the mines fields. Engr. Sluice would not ignore this.

ഇരു

One day as Engr. Sluice was passing through the gate to his office, Mr. Uduak was following him behind. As he was parking his car, Uduak was also parking his. Engr. Sluice looked and discovered it was him.

"Mr. Uduak you never care to check on me since last time our appointment failed. How is the mining operation?"

"Well, we are trying our best as usual. It is better than doing nothing."

"That is the usual language of rich people like you. You hardly say things are moving fine," Engr. Sluice said.

"Inspector, let us go to your office first. You will know why I said so." They entered the office.

"The reason that we could not hold the appointment we fixed the other time was because my vehicle spoiled at Udawa while on my way to Birnin Gwari for mineral samples. I couldn't come back in good time."

"I was in the workshop of Baba Kekere when you called him that day. He stopped repairing my vehicle and left immediately to attend to you. As soon as he left, my Mines Manager called to tell me that there was a problem in my mine. I had to rush there."

"What was the problem?" Engr. Sluice asked, thinking of how the activities of drug couriers were tarnishing the corporate image of Nigeria internationally. He had listened to some news on that from the radio as he was coming to the office that morning.

"There is a road the villagers use to their farms and I blocked it since it passes the area of my Mining Lease. That day the youths went to the site and insisted they must pass through my Lease to their farms even to the extent of removing the obstruction I put across the road. We arranged to be here today with Mallam Danyaro, their Chief, on this matter. I believe he will soon be here. I can hear the sound of a car outside. It may be him. Yes, he is the one. That is his voice," Mr. Uduak recognized the voice of Mallam Danyaro as he greeted Jegede outside while heading to the office of Engr. Sluice.

"Chief, you are a little bit late," Mr. Uduak observed.

"I was delayed by a traffic jam. I am sorry for being late, please."

"It is alright, Chief. How are your people?" Engr. Sluice asked.

"They are well but they are giving Mr. Uduak trouble. We are here for that. I believe Mr. Uduak might have briefed you on that."

"He was just doing that when you arrived."

"So, what can we do now? I want my people and Mr. Uduak to be at peace. That is the only major road to our farms even before my grandfather was born and now Mr. Uduak says we will not use the road because it passes through his area of digging the mine – mine -," he could not pronounce it fully.

"Mineral," Engr. Sluice helped him.

"Yes, mi-ne-ral."

"Don't worry, Chief. Mr. Uduak will allow you and your people to use the road that is older than all of you in the village."

"No! Not all of us! We still have one old man who has refused to die and he is now blind. He grew up seeing our ancestors using another road and not this present one which was constructed in his days. They abandoned the previous one because it passed through a hill with a lengthy but not very steep slope. It was not easy for the people to use it. They only endured it. The story has it that some white men used to come to the hill and dug some stones, beautiful stones that were green and blue. They used our people to dig the stones for them. One man picked such a

180

stone along a river bed. A white man gave the man five British pounds sterling at that time when money had great value and collected it from him. The man used the money to build the first zinc house in our village. It is still standing up till today. It is being used, conserved and preserved as a historical piece."

"Mr. Uduak, he is speaking about the gems. They could be green and blue tourmaline," Engr. Sluice said.

"Oh, yes; no doubt about that," Mr. Uduak responded, already thinking of applying for a mineral title over the area. But it had been unknowingly covered to that extent by another company with Exploration Licence of over 650 cadastral units. The company drew up the site plan for the application of the Exploration Licence from a topographical sheet without having carried out a field survey of the site and was yet to place demarcation markers to know the extent of the coverage of the Licence. However, Mr. Uduak might still succeed if he plays his part very well as the consent letter with which the mining company used to get the Exploration Licence was not given by the community of Gidan Mutum Daya as stipulated in Section 100 of the Act, thus;

'When an application is made for a mineral title in respect of an area ... the notice of the application shall be given in the prescribed manner to the owner or occupier of the land and consent obtained before the licence is granted, otherwise the licence may be granted with exclusion of the private land in question.'

The mining company that had the Exploration Licence over the area used the consent letter from a community whose jurisdiction did not extend to the community of Gidan Mutum Daya. Therefore, its

Licence coverage of the lands of Gidan Mutum Daya was null and void. Under this ground, Mr. Uduak, or any other person who duly obtained the consent of the owner(s) or occupier(s) of the hill and its environs, could have the application for the Licence approved by the Mining Cadastre Office if all other things remain equal after the revocation of the part thereof in the Licence of the company that had wrongly covered the area. However, Mr. Uduak would have to launder his image which has been tarnished by the ongoing prevention of the community's freedom of passage through the area of his Lease by listening to the statutory advice Engr. Sluice will soon give to him.

"Will Mr. Uduak allow peace to reign by allowing my people to use the road?" the Chief asked, looking worried as he neither liked to hurt his people nor Mr. Uduak by taking side with any of the two parties. He knew, even though Mr. Uduak's mining activities will benefit the community socially and economically, one day he will leave the area. He would be left with his people whom he ought to stand for, come rain, come sunshine, as a good leader should. Therefore, it was a delicate situation that needed caution of the highest order to handle just like in any other conflict resolution worldwide.

"Yes, he will allow your people to use the road. He needs your co-operation to work there. I will talk to him. You may wish to leave now as I know you have some other things to do," he said.

"Thank you. I must go now. Mr. Uduak, co-operate with the Inspector. Inspector, I am waiting to hear from you of the outcome of your discussion with him," the Chief said and left.

"Don't worry, everything will be alright," Engr. Sluice assured him and wished him safe journey.

Engr. Sluice sighed heavily and Mr. Uduak asked him why he did so.

"Mr. Uduak, I am surprised and worried how people would not obey the mining laws. Section 33(8) of the Regulations has made it clear that '*the area of a Reconnaissance permit include all land within the territory of Nigeria available for mining operations*' excluding areas covered by any other mineral title as spelt out in Section 33(9) of the Regulations."

"And what is happening, Inspector?"

"Sir Louise, your tribal man, is using his prospector to carry out reconnaissance survey for columbite, taking samples here and there, in the area of the Mining Lease of Messrs Mining for Nigeria Progress Plc. I have warned him to stop doing that but he would not listen. My hands are tied on how to deal with him as I may not be supported by Abuja if I get him arrested."

"Why?"

"He was a course mate of the Permanent Secretary in the University. They schooled overseas. He goes to Abuja from time to time to see him. I am in a dilemma. I don't know, I don't know; aaaaaaaa."

"Your Permanent Secretary, the one I know, is a no nonsense man; he will not support him to do a bad thing. Do your work as you ought to without any fear. Abuja will be behind you. However, if Abuja is not, let me know. He is my close friend, I mean your Permanent Secretary," Mr. Uduak boasted.

"Go and draft a letter to the Divisional Police Officer and ask for his support to go and arrest Sir Luis next tomorrow," Engr. Sluice told Johnson who had just entered his office to inform him that one company had disposed minerals obtained in the course of exploration without seeking permission from the office and paying royalty as prescribed in Section 137(1) of the Regulations and Section 63 of the Act. He didn't know Engr. Sluice was with someone.

"Okay, sir," Johnson said and left.

"Now, Mr. Uduak, on your problem with the community of Gidan Mutum Daya, the law is not on your side. You will have to allow the people to use the road."

"Which law says so? I don't want to hear this, Engr. Sluice!"

"Wait and listen to this," Engr. Sluice said and picked up the Act and opened to Section 83 and read thus;

'No person shall, except in relation to minerals designated by the Minister as strategic in accordance with the provisions of this Act, in the course of explorations or carrying on mining operations under this Act impede or obstruct the right of way over any public road.'

"This is very clear to everybody. Obey the law and allow them to use the road. After all, you need peace to work the mine successfully. More so, where you are working is not in any way close to that road. You must understand this, please."

"No problem; I need them and they need me as someone would say *'right hand washes left hand; left hand washes right hand.'* That is my situation with the community," Mr. Uduak succumbed and sighed.

"Why did you sigh? Are you having a second thought on this matter?" Engr. Sluice asked.

"Not, at all. Who am I to go against the law?"

"So, what is it that is the matter with you?"

"I used to have an emerald Small Scale Mining Lease in Nasarawa State, the home of solid

184

minerals; you know that is the slogan for the state. I decided, after two years of working there, to surrender it in accordance with the provisions of Section 96 of the Regulations as I thought that the place was not profitable. Now the person that was granted the place after the surrender has a good return on investment there. He has struck an extensive vein of the emerald. Patience is very important."

"Yes, it is," Engr. Sluice responded.

"Inspector, our friend, the Chairman of Join the Family of Miners Ltd. wants to transfer or assign his Reconnaissance Permit to another company," Mr. Uduak said.

"That is not possible. Unlike other mineral titles, Reconnaissance Permit cannot be transferred or assigned to anyone or company as prohibited by Section 91(3) of the Regulations."

"Is that so?"

"Yes, it is so!"

"Inspector, I want to submit another application over the area of my Exploration Licence revoked 12 months ago. I like that place very well."

"You can't do that as the former title holder over the area until after 2 years from the date of revocation of the Licence. That is the provision of Section 35(17)(a) of the Regulations. Pray that another person will not submit an application over the place within the 2 years. You were careless not to have fulfilled your obligations and now you are crying over the area."

"Do not mind me, Inspector. I won't do that again. I want to go now. I have to go and see what is happening at the site."

"That is good. I won't be able to see you off; safe journey."

As Mr. Uduak was going out of the office, Engr. Sluice sat silently, thinking about a case reported to the office by Nigeria Inland Waterways Authority (NIWA) concerning gravel bailing operations from a river bed. He sent for Johnson.

"Johnson, I will fix a date for us to go to River Kaduna in the locality of Maje to find out how the sand is being dredged there. NIWA has reported that there is a problem of how it is being done; here is the letter of complaint; file it in the NIWA file," he said and cast his mind back to the Asaba section of River Niger, imagining how anchored mobile dredgers were dredging out sand.

"Johnson, Mr. Akintola will not escape paying a fine not exceeding twenty million naira (₦20,000,000;00) or an imprisonment of a term not exceeding five (5) years or both for contravening the provisions on environmental compliance as stated in Section 20(7)(1) of the Regulations. He had disregarded compliance with environmental laws with impunity. He will face the consequences as the Director of Mines Environmental Compliance will not tolerate this. Now, you can go

TWELVE

Engr. Sluice sat quietly in his office as if he was thinking of a solution to an engineering problem which he had once encountered at a mine, but that was not what was going on in his mind. He was recalling the several encounters he previously had during the numerous field inspection trips that he had recently undertaken. He recalled the following happenings: how Manir and Dankano escaped from the Zumunci Mining Camp; how the old man at Zumunci Mining Camp had a gun with him; how illegal marital unions were going on in illegal mining camps; how the illegal miners were always scheming against one another; how the armed bandits harassed them in Zumunci Mining Camp. Others are the violent encounters between miners and host communities; the erection of huts in the illegal mining camps; the sprouting of markets in the illegal mining camps; mining companies having difficulties in always complying with the provisions of the mining laws; mines collapsing and killing miners; how Mines Officers were normally exposed to dangers from people, wild animals like the lion and python, weather elements and rugged terrains, sometimes with heavy woods or rivers to pass through; his meeting with people of different cultures in the course of official duties; how the Mining Laws came to bear on the different and interesting scenarios in the mines fields and many other things such as the huge financial and social benefits attached to mining and other associated dangers .He concluded that the experiences were both interesting and nasty like thorny flowers that are beautiful to behold yet they are nasty and he laughed and said it would be good for someone to write a book titled '**Nigerian Mining Laws in Thorny Flowers.**' Indeed, as he went round to enforce compliance of the mining laws, he had such thorny but flowery experiences.

"Alice," Engr. Sluice called after he had stopped relishing on the thorny and the flowery field experiences.

"Yes, sir," she answered in high spirits. That morning, Engr. Sluice had approved an application for her annual leave to enable her go with the father to the island of Madagascar to visit an aunty.

"Alice, tell Johnson and Maxwell to come to my office. Bassey should also come with them." Bassey had just been transferred from the South-South zone to the North-West zone.

As Alice left to call them, Engr. Sluice received a phone call from the Director of Mines Inspectorate.

"Engr. Sluice, I have gone through your letter concerning Jungle Mining Limited's refusal to pay Chief Okafor compensation for the destruction of the economic trees in his land. Jungle Mining Ltd was granted the mineral title over one year ago. This is a violation of the provisions of Section 109(1)(a) of the Act by not paying the compensation within six months of the grant of the mineral title.

"Sir, aaa…"

"Just listen to me, Sluice. Write a letter and demand from him the payment of the compensation within one week or he will face the suspension of his mineral title."

"Okay, sir."

"Yes, let him know that if he does not pay the compensation after 30 days from the date of eventual suspension, the Minister may revoke the mineral title in compliance with the provisions of Section 109(1)(c) of the Act. Keep me updated on the development about this matter. I have learned that Chief Okafor is considering seeing the Minister on that. We must not give room for the Minister to think we are not doing our work. Management will not listen to any complaint on lack of logistics. I know you will complain on this. Your job delivery must not suffer in any way. Do you get me, Engr. Sluice?"

"I do, sir."

"That is good; do your work without fear or favour. Another thing I want to tell you is that the Permanent Secretary may be on a three day working visit together with the Director of Artisanal and Small Scale Mining Department(ASM) to your zone in two week's time. You must be ready to receive them."

"Okay, sir."

"Do you remember that the community of Danhuta has written to him, complaining of sand quarrying operators destroying their lands by the river side? He is from that village and may wish to visit the area. Therefore, get yourself equipped to explain to him the actions you have taken. You must show yourself competent to handle the zone. I trust you can do well."

"No problem, sir."

"Be in-charge of any circumstance that may arise; be confident and eat up any circumstance that may confront you; okay?"

"I understand, sir," he answered, flipping through the pages of the Act without having any Section of it in mind to read. He was just doing that in pleasure with his mind attentive to the Director.

"That is all I want to tell you," the Director, Mines Inspectorate, concluded and Engr. Sluice heard him from the background telling somebody that he would soon go on a surprise tour of the zone. Engr. Sluice laughed and said *"you* (the Director) *will not find me wanting no matter what."*

೫)ೞ

Johnson, Maxwell and Bassey came to answer Engr. Sluice's call.

"Why do you look dull, Bassey?" Engr. Sluice asked while he was calling the Chairman of one of the mining co-operatives on phone to tell him that he should get his members informed that the Director of ASM may likely have an interactive session with them as he accompanies the Permanent Secretary on his working visit to the zone with a view to hearing from them about their operational bottlenecks. The Director of ASM has severally visited Zamfara State to interact with artisanal miners. They had been encouraged by his visits and kept on expecting more of the visits. This time around, the mining co-operatives in Kaduna might be fortunate to have him for the first time.

"There is nothing, sir; I am okay," Bassey answered.

"All of you sit down; I want to find out how much you know about the Mining Laws and other things. Each one of you will answer five questions. Each question carries twenty (20) percent (%). Alice, sit down and record their scores."

"Johnson, after fulfilling the requirements for commencement of mining operations, within how many months should a Mining Lease title holder commence mining operations in his site?"

"Within 36 calendar months," Johnson answered. He was correct because that is what Section 118(2)(a) of the Regulations says.

"That is correct. You have scored 20%.

"Maxwell, within how many months should the holder of a Small Scale Mining Lease commence mining operations after fulfilling the requirements for commencement of the mining operations? Bring the copy of the Regulations in your hand. I don't want you to steal the answer from it. You guys of these days are negatively too smart for my liking."

"The answer is three (3) calendar months from the date of issuance of the mineral title!" Maxwell answered with excitement as a primary school pupil, and he was correct as Section 118(2)(d) says so.

"Maxwell, I thought you would not get it; you have scored 20%! That is good.

"Now, Bassey, it is your turn. Given that a company has fulfilled all the requirements on an Exploration Licence for the commencement of work, within how many months should the company start the exploration activities?"

"Twelve (12) Calendar months; yes, twelve calendar months." Maxwell laughed at Bassey, thinking the answer was ten (10) months but he was wrong. Bassey was right.

"Bassey you got it! 20% for you," Engr. Sluice announced.

"Bassey, let me start from you now. Listen very well. State one requirement for commencement of work by any mineral title holder as prescribed by Section 118 on pre-conditions for commencement of mining operations."

"One of the requirements is payment of royalty!" Bassey answered, still bathing in the pool of excitement for answering the first question correctly. He was wrong this time.

"Capital NO; you have gotten it wrong this time. 0%."

"Now, to you, Maxwell; pay attention. State one requirement a company has to fulfill as a pre-condition for starting mining operations."

Maxwell hesitated to answer. Initially, he wanted to say clearing of the site and later said submission of an approved Environmental Impact Assessment (EIA) and a plan of how to stop pollution of the environment to Mines Environmental Compliance Department, and he got it as it is stated in Section 118(1)(i) of the Regulations.

"Another 20% to Maxwell!"

"Now, Johnson, having fulfilled all the requirements for commencement of mining activities, within how many months should the holder of a quarry lease commences the quarrying operations?"

Johnson showed a sign of not being sure of the answer by scratching his head as if that would bring out the answer and said 5 months.

"You are wrong, Johnson. Six (6) calendar months is the right answer. Open to Section 118(2)(c) of the Regulations and you will see that. You have 0%. Now let us continue.

"I start from you, Johnson. What is a security mineral as defined by the Act?"

"It is a radioactive mineral that has 0.05% of uranium or thorium, or any combination of ...."

"You have tried very well. You have scored18%. Bassey read the definition of security mineral in Section 164, last paragraph of page 60 of the Act," he said and gave him a copy of the Act.

'Security mineral means a radioactive mineral which contains by weight at least one twentieth of one percent (0.05%) of the uranium, thorium, or any combination thereof including but not limited to monozite, sand and other ores containing thorium, caronite, pitch blend and other ores containing uranium,' Bassey read but not as Maxwell would have.

"You guys must have this in your head.

"Now, Maxwell, it is your turn; after blasting operations in a quarry, who should be the first person to go to the quarry face?"

"It is the short-firer (the blaster)."

"You got it again! That is what Section 47 of the Explosives Regulations says; another 20% for you!" Engr. Sluice said, beginning to change his negative perception of Maxwell concerning his knowledge of the mining laws. He turned to throw a question at Bassey.

"Bassey, what is a misfire?"

Bassey had just read Section 48-54 of the Explosives Regulations on misfire and how to treat it the previous day.

"It is unexploded explosives in a drill hole after blasting operations due to a misfired detonator."

"You are correct! 20% to you; that is what Sections 51 and 54 of the Explosives Regulations explained.

"Now, starting from you again, Bassey; "at the beginning of a month, the stock of high explosives in a magazine of a certain company was 2000kg. During the month the company used 1005 kg and transferred 505kg to another of its quarry. What is the remaining quantity of the explosives should the company reflect in its explosives returns at the end of the month in compliance with Section 63(1)(d) of the Explosives Regulations?"

It took Bassey about 45 seconds to say 489kg." He nearly got it but was not very careful.

"Four hundred and ninety (490) kg is the right answer. Your answer is short of 1kg and you know 1kg of explosives is enough to cause an enormous havoc should it falls into the hands of dangerous elements in the society of today. No marks for you this time around. Bassey; you have scored 0%. Let us move on.

"Maxwell, define a metal."

"It is a chemical element or elements physically combined which have some or all of the following properties: malleability, ductility, hardness, strength, solidity and is good conductor of heat and electricity."

"This day is yours! You got it! 20% for you, Maxwell!

"Now, Johnson; what is the maximum life span for mineral titles apart from Water Use Permit?"

"For the initial issuance, Small Scale Mining Lease is 5 years; Quarry Lease, 5 years; Reconnaissance Permit, 1 year; Exploration Licence, 3 years; and Mining Lease, 25 years."

"You have got it! 20% for you; I hope all of you know that the life-span of Water Use Permit is the same with any of the mineral titles for which use it was granted subject to the validity of the mineral title. Section 81 of the Regulations says so. Now, we are coming to the end of this quiz. This is the fifth and the last round.

"Now, Johnson, I will ask you and I am sure you will get the answer. Since the inception of the

Mining Cadastre Office, name the Director-Generals of that Agency till date."

"They are Professor Ibrahim Garba, Engr. Obadiah S. Nkom and Engr. M. K. Amate who is the current Director-General."

"Engr. Obadiah S. Nkom has never occupied that seat; perhaps he will, one day. You are wishing him well. For now, he is the Director of Concessions in the Agency. The third person you missed is the tall Sheik Mohammed Goni! For missing one person, you got 13.33%.

"To you Maxwell; name the present and the immediate two past Directors of Mines Inspectorate?"

"The present Director is acting. He is K.F. Wuyep: the immediate two past Directors were Engr. Dauda Awolowo and Engr. Umar Idris."

"Maxwell, each of the names mentioned correctly attracts 6.66%; you got two correctly that is 13.32%; the third one is Engr. Dauda Awojobi and not Engr. Dauda Awolowo. Instead of 6.66% on him, you have 3.33%; your mark for this question is therefore, 16.65%.

"Finally, Bassey, mention the names of the present Directors for Mines Inspectorate, Mines Environmental Compliance and Artisanal and Small-Scale Mining Departments."

"K. F. Wuyep for Mines Inspectorate, Engr. Sallim A. Salaam for Mines Environmental Compliance and Mr. Patrick Ojukwu for ASM."

"You missed one name; that of the ASM Department. He is Mr. Patrick Ojeka and not Patrick Ojukwu. On this note, you have 13.32%.

We have come to the end of this exciting quiz which I hope will provoke you to study the Act, the Regulations and other policy instruments of the

Ministry to show yourself approved Mines Officers who rightly administered the mining laws. You know you must be competent even before going to arrest illegal miners. This will make you effective or you will be put to shame to the annoyance of the Minister or the Director, Legal Department and the Director, Mines Inspectorate Department, who expect us to know the law very well as we perform our duties.

"It is time to listen to your scores; Alice, over to you."

Alice read their scores round by round and the total for each was as follows:

S/NO	JOHNSON	MAXWELL	BASSEY
1	20%	20%	20%
2	0%	20%	0%
3	18%	20%	20%
4	20%	20%	0%
5	13.33%	16.65%	13.32%
TOTAL	71.33%	96.65%	53.32%

"Now everybody has heard the results," Engr. Sluice said. "All of you have tried. Johnson and Bassey, you need to do more next time." He kept quiet for a moment and then said, "The reason for giving you this quiz is to determine who will be sent to Australia for a course on their mining laws next week. That was the instruction form the Director of Mines. By the results, Maxwell will represent our zone in this rare trip which will be sponsored by the Australian Government. The two of you, Johnson and Bassey, anyone of you that does well next time will go since it is an annual sponsorship. Maxwell, I hope your international passport has not expired?" A former

Zonal Mines Officer had advised them to have international passports incase of times like this.

"It has not, sir," he answered, bubbling with unspeakable joy. He had never traveled by air before.

"Maxwell, Maxwell," Alice called, admiring her trouble-making friend and wondering how he could be this intelligent because he was often restless. "You must bring something for me from Australia," she said and knocked Maxwell on the head once and said again, "stubborn, troublesome but bright" to the further demoralization of Johnson and Bassey.

Engr. Sluice turned and looked at his Switzerland made wrist watch and discovered there was no more time to go to River Kaduna that day to meet the officers of the Nigerian Inland Water Ways (NIWA). He decided to call to tell them to reschedule the appointment. However, he wondered why they asked the sand quarrying operators along the channel of River Kaduna to establish a stable river bed and bank profile so as not to '*substantially alter river currents or change erosion and deposition patterns downstream*' in compliance with the provisions of Section 167 of the Regulations since River Kaduna was not a navigable water way. The local inhabitants that used wooden boats had not made a complaint on that. Therefore, to him the sand quarrying operators had not contravened the provisions of Section 78(5) of the Act which he asked Maxwell to read thus;

'*Nothing in this Section shall authorize the holder of a quarry lease to make such alterations in the flow of water in any navigable water as would obstruct or interfere with the free and safe passage of any vessel, boat, canoe or other craft,*' Maxwell read, slightly pronouncing words as a white man in preparation for his trip to Australia.

"*Shege*, Maxwell; you have not even gone there and you have begun to speak like them. *Na wa* for you. You cannot stop this funny attitude of yours," Alice said.

"All of you should leave my office now. The three of you should see me together by 10am tomorrow," he said and remembered he had to go to Messrs Allow Everybody In Limited site. The company's lease had expired. It had not paid surface rent to the traditional ruler of the host community and it had an outstanding royalty to pay to the government. It was removing all its plants and buildings from the site. As Engr. Sluice was thinking of going to the site, Jegede came to his office.

"Jegede, we are going to the mining site of Allow Everybody In Limited now-now. Go and bring the car quickly."

"Okay, sir," he said. He went and brought the car and off they went.

⁊ʘ

As they approached the site of Messrs Allow Everybody In Limited, they saw many people quarreling. It was the Site Manager of the company and his staff who were quarrelling with the host community. The host community was preventing them from removing the plants and buildings at the site.

"That is the Inspector of mineral coming. Let him come and tell us whether what this company is doing is correct. How can the company leave this place without paying surface rent to the Chief?"

⁊ʘ

"Inspector, thank God you are here. This company must pay me the surface rent before it will be allowed to remove its properties from this land," the Chief said.

"Our Managing Director said even if the company leaves now, the surface rent will be paid later."

"No, we won't agree," the children of the Chief objected. Others joined, "yes, we will not agree."

"Everybody should be quiet. Site Manager, stop your people from removing any of your belongings. Your company must pay the surface rent to the Chief and the outstanding royalty of Two Million, Nine Hundred and Fifty thousand Naira (₦2,950,000.00) to the government or your assets will be treated in accordance with the provisions of Section 74(2)(c) of the Regulations by declaring them the properties of the Federal Government and shall be '*disposed of in lieu of the rent*' and the royalty."

"That will be good for us, Inspector," the children of the Chief said.

"Yes, that is what the law says," Engr. Sluice concluded and said he would engage the services of the police to guard the site against the company removing anything from it.

֍Ձ

The following morning, Engr. Sluice met with Johnson, Maxwell and Bassey in his office.

"You are all aware that I will soon take my exit from the civil service of the nation. I am grateful to the Almighty God and this nation for the glorious opportunity to serve her. Throughout the years of my service of this great nation, my guiding principle is love for this nation with the hope that one day it will move from a third world to a first world status as did

Singapore. I besiege all of you to love this country. Forget vested interests. I have this token for you." He said, holding a document in his hand. "This will help you a lot in carrying out your duties. I have been grooming all of you to be sound so that you help in the management of the Mines Inspectorate Department based on sound knowledge of the mining laws…," he continued and gave each of them a copy of the document. It was a list of corresponding Sections of the Act and the Regulations as shown below.

SUBJECT MATTER	SECTION(S) OF THE ACT.	CORRESPONDING SECTION(S) OF THE REGULATINS.
Compensation	107-13, 125, 160(4,5)	11-12, 154
Surface rent	102	100
Revocation of mineral titles.	11,12,126(4), 151 – 156	97
Annual service fee	10(b)	98
Mineral Resources and Environmental Management Committee (MIREMCO)	19	155
Royalty on minerals won during mining.	33	123,99
Royalty on minerals won from exploration activities.	63	137
Solid Minerals Development Fund.	34-42	19
Discovery of additional mineral(s) not in the mineral title.	64	88

mineral title		
Abandonment or permanent cessation of production	159	95, 128, 217-218
Technical competence for mineral title	54, 73	26, 139
Competitive bidding of mineral titles	9	4
Licence to purchase and possess minerals	92-94	133
Working capital or financial capability	54	27
Obligations of Exploration Licence (EL) holder	61	42, 111
Obligations of Mining Lease (ML) holder	70	114
Discovery of radioactive minerals	44	129
Restoration or reclamation of mines land	114 – 115, 118(b), 128	156
Boundary lines of a mineral title defined	145	108
Survey of a mineral title	79	28
Export of mineral samples for analysis	60(1)(e), 144	132

"I will write a comprehensive report on my recent inspection tour of mining sites in the zone and forward it to Abuja. Finally, and I repeat, finally, manage the mines fields with professionalism so as to reposition the mining industry in line with the vision and the mission statements of the Ministry in spite of the thorns for the economic and others (flowery) benefits of all stakeholders. You can go now."

They all left silently. They were visibly touched by his words which would be more powerful on the day he retires when people will gather to celebrate him for serving the country for many years.

www.ingramcontent.com/pod-product-compliance
Lightning Source LLC
Chambersburg PA
CBHW031953170626
46807CB00006B/2466